"Please . . . don't jump!"

I shielded my eyes from the sun.

And then I saw him. A teenage boy. Wearing jeans and a yellow T-shirt. He was standing over the falls. Right on the edge.

I gasped . . . I hadn't expected him to be standing there.

He didn't see me. He was staring straight down, down to the jagged black rocks below the falling water.

He took a step forward.

My heart stopped.

I realized what he was about to do.

"Stop!" I screamed. "Don't jump! Please . . . don't jump!"

Don't miss other Scholastic thrillers
by R.L. Stine:

The Baby-sitter
The Baby-sitter II
The Baby-sitter III
The Hitchhiker
The Girlfriend
The Boyfriend
Beach House
Beach Party
Hit and Run
The Snowman
Twisted
Blind Date

R.L. STINE

THE DEAD GIRLFRIEND

SCHOLASTIC INC.
New York Toronto London Auckland Sydney

No part of this publication may be reproduced in whole or in part, or stored in a retrieval system, or transmitted in any form or by any means, electronic, mechanical, photocopying, recording, or otherwise, without written permission of the publisher. For information regarding permission, write to Scholastic Inc., 730 Broadway, New York, NY 10003.

ISBN 0-590-45387-4

12 11 10 9 8 7 6 5 4 3 2 1   3 4 5 6 7 8/9

Printed in the U.S.A.   01

First Scholastic printing, August 1993

THE DEAD GIRLFRIEND

Chapter 1

The first time I saw Jonathan Morgan, he terrified me.

I probably should have known then — at that very first moment, staring into the sun at him from my bike — to stay away.

Danger here.

Danger and fear.

I think I knew at that moment that Jonathan meant trouble. But a person doesn't always listen to these signals. A person doesn't always listen to her sensible self. At least, I didn't.

And before I knew it, I found myself trapped by Jonathan.

Caught up in his sadness. Caught up in his mystery.

A mystery that began in murder.

It all started on such a beautiful day, warm and promising, fresh as only a day in late April can be.

I borrowed my brother Kenny's bike and went riding. I wanted to explore Shocklin Falls, our new home.

Kenny's bike was a clunky BMX, heavy and slow, and the seat was too high for me. (Do you *believe* I'm shorter than my little brother? It's so annoying.) But my 21-speed had been stolen just before we moved. So what choice did I have?

I'm sixteen and I have my driver's license. But you can't really explore in a car.

Bike riding is my passion. I love the rush of wind against my face, the feel of the pedals under my sneakers, the control, the way it makes my legs throb and my heart pound.

The total *freedom* of it.

You can't feel that in a car.

Dad promised I could buy a new bike as soon as the insurance company paid for the stolen one. I really didn't want to wait that long. But Dad wasn't in any mood for arguments.

He and Mom are still unpacking cartons. I think they'll be unpacking cartons until next Christmas! You just don't realize how much *stuff* a family of four owns until you move to a new town.

Anyway, I took off on Kenny's bike. I'm such a shrimp. I should've lowered the seat. But I was too impatient to get away and explore Shocklin Falls.

I was wearing green Lycra bike shorts and a bright blue sleeveless T-shirt. It was the first really warm spring day, and the afternoon sun felt hot on my back.

I had just washed my hair, which is long and blonde and very straight. I had tied it behind my head with a blue ribbon. I knew the sun would dry it.

The air smelled so sweet! All down my street, the dogwood trees had blossomed. It was like riding under majestic white arches, so pretty and unreal.

Prettier than real life, I thought.

I get these kinds of thoughts when I'm out bike riding.

It didn't take too long to explore Shocklin Falls. It's a very small town. The community college where Mom and Dad are going to start teaching next semester is at one end. Then come quiet streets, shady under rows of old trees, lined with small, nice-looking houses.

The big, expensive houses are out by the falls on the other side of town. And in the middle is a small shopping district — two-story buildings, mostly, a two-screen movie theater, a bank, and a post office. Not much else. The nearest mall is in Cedar, two towns away.

I rode slowly past the small shops. For a Saturday afternoon, the town wasn't very crowded. I think most people were home doing spring-cleaning, working on their gardens and yards.

An old station wagon rumbled past, filled with teenagers, its windows open, radio blaring an old Def Leppard song. The noise drew frowns and headshakes from two elderly women about to cross Main Street arm in arm.

A bike shop on the corner of Main and Walnut caught my eye. I climbed off Kenny's bike and walked it up to the front window. I pressed my nose against the glass, peering inside. Looked like a pretty good selection. I'd definitely have to check it out later.

I climbed back onto Kenny's bike and coasted unsteadily off the curb back onto the street. Is that all there is to town? I wondered.

Yep. I'd seen it all.

I circled the block once again, then headed toward the falls.

I hadn't seen the famous falls yet. Mrs. Pratte, the real estate agent who sold us our house, couldn't stop raving about how beautiful and spectacular they are.

So I was saving the best part of my tour for last.

Mrs. Pratte described the falls as rising up high on a sheer rock cliff, then cascading straight down like a steamy, white curtain into the wide Monohonka River below.

She was good at describing things, which I guess you need to be if you're going to sell real estate. Anyway, she said it was as pretty as Niagara Falls, except much smaller, of course, and you could see three towns from up at the top.

I followed Main Street past the shopping district and soon found myself in the fancy part of Shocklin Falls. Big houses. Some of them looked like *mansions* to me! A lot of them had teams of gardeners out working in the yards, planting beds of flowers and weeding and clearing away the dead leaves.

I had a little scare when a snarling German shepherd came bounding after me. Its owner was yelling for the dog to come back, but of course the dog paid no attention.

I began pedaling furiously, standing up to get better speed. Luckily, the dog gave up after two-thirds of a block and contented itself to end the chase and bark out a warning for me to stay away.

"Okay, okay. I can take a hint!" I called back to it, still pedaling standing up.

The big houses gave way to woods. The trees

were still mostly bare, the spring leaves just beginning to open. A squirrel scampered up a tree, startled by my silent, gliding intrusion.

I found the bike path Mrs. Pratte had described. It curved through the woods, climbing higher as it went, becoming steeper and steeper as it made its way up through the thick trees.

After about a ten-minute ride, I found myself at the top. I was pleased to see that I wasn't at all out of breath. Being in good shape is really important to me. It's one reason I always prefer my bike to a car.

I kept pedaling. The woods were all to my right now. To my left — the steep cliff edge, a sheer drop to black rocks below.

I slowed down. There was no guardrail or anything. At some points, the dirt bike path came within a foot or two of the cliff edge. And the path was really curvy.

I heard the falls before I saw them. A soft, steady roar that grew louder as I approached.

And then the path curved, and the falls were right in front of me.

How can I describe them? They were dazzling.

The white water fell straight down, sparkling like a million diamonds, splashing back up in a shimmery white mist.

Looking down, I could see the wide brown river flowing between green banks. And I could see far into the distance, over trees, over fields. I could see the town, tiny like a miniature, and beyond it another town, and then, in the misty distance, a third town.

I slowed to a stop. The bike path ended abruptly at a tall pile of gray granite rocks.

I shielded my eyes from the sun.

And then I saw him.

A teenage boy. Wearing jeans and a yellow T-shirt. He was standing over the falls. Right on the edge.

I gasped and gripped the handlebars. I hadn't expected anyone to be standing there.

He didn't see me. He was staring straight down, down to the jagged black rocks below the falling water.

He looks like Luke Perry, I thought.

He had the same James Dean-style flattop.

But I didn't have much time to think about his looks.

Still staring straight down, he took a step forward.

My heart stopped.

I realized what he was about to do.

"Stop!" I screamed, trying to be heard over the roar of the falls. "Don't jump! Please — don't jump!"

Chapter 2

He cried out and stepped back.

My screams had startled him.

I jumped off the bike and hurried toward him. The bike clattered onto the rocks behind me.

"Hey — " he called. His expression changed from surprise to confusion. He jammed his hands into his jeans pockets and he moved away from the edge, toward me.

He was tall and very handsome. He did look like Luke Perry. He had sideburns, too. He was really tanned. He had a cleft chin. He stared at me with striking green eyes.

I guess I was staring hard at him. That's how I managed to see his face so clearly.

"I thought you were someone else," he said, shouting over the sound of the falls. He smiled. A crooked smile, but very handsome.

I think I fell in love with him then. Or something like that. I'm not sure. It's impossible to explain. I was so embarrassed about shouting like that.

"I thought you were going to — " I started, but I didn't want to finish my sentence.

He was still smiling, hands jammed into his pockets, his yellow T-shirt fluttering in the wind. "You what?"

"I'm sorry," I stammered. "I saw you at the edge, and . . ."

I get a slight stammer whenever I'm really nervous. And believe me, I was really stammering now!

He laughed. He had a great laugh. Sort of tossed his head back and crinkled those incredible green eyes.

"You thought I was going to jump?" The smile faded. His eyes burned into mine, studying me.

I nodded. I could feel my face turn red.

I tugged at my hair. It was still wet.

"I'm just waiting for someone," he said. "Looks like they're not coming."

"I — I've never been up here before," I stammered, lowering my eyes. I didn't like standing there. I don't normally have trouble with heights. But we were so high up, and the drop was so straight, so steep, and the rocks below looked so sharp and pointed.

"You go to Shocklin High?" he asked.

I shook my head. "Starting Monday. We just moved here. From Ohio. I'm Annie Kiernan," I said awkwardly. I always find it so hard to introduce myself like that. I don't know why.

"Jonathan Morgan," he said. He removed his hands from his jeans pockets and shook my hand. Very formal.

He grinned.

I loved the cleft in his chin. And I loved the way the wind blew through his hair but it stayed standing up, every hair in place.

I should have seen the sadness in those green eyes.

I should have seen the fear. The dread.

But of course I didn't.

I should have asked him why he was standing right on the cliff edge like that, staring down so intently into the crashing waters.

But of course I didn't.

Instead, I said, "It's so awesome up here." Pretty lame, but at least I had stopped stammering.

"Yeah," he replied, scratching his right sideburn.

"The town is so ordinary," I went on. "I mean, it's okay. But it's nothing special. You don't expect to find something like this." I motioned to the falls.

Jonathan's eyes were on the woods behind me. "I . . . uh . . . left my bike back there," he said. "Wait right here. I'll go get it."

"You like to bike ride?" I asked as he headed past me.

"Yeah. A lot," he called back without stopping. He disappeared behind the wide pile of granite rocks.

I wrapped my arms around my chest and stared out at the town below. Even with the afternoon sun high above, it was a little chilly up there.

What a fabulous spot, I thought.

I knew I'd be riding my bike up there often.

I suddenly wondered if I'd be riding it beside Jonathan. I had this silly idea that we were fated to meet up there. Like an old black-and-white romantic movie.

Maybe I'll ask him to go riding next weekend or something, I thought.

I saw him approaching, walking a sleek black racing bike.

No. He must have a girlfriend, I realized, a sinking feeling in my stomach.

He's too good-looking not to have a girlfriend.

He said he was meeting someone up there.

He leaned his bike against one of the big stones and made his way over the dirt toward me, taking long, slow strides. "So you just moved here?" he asked, pulling a long strand of grass from my hair.

"Yeah. My parents are going to teach at Logan. You know. The community college."

"Weird time to move," he said, staring over my shoulder at the falls.

"Tell me about it," I groaned. "Changing schools and everything. It's horrible!"

He gazed at me thoughtfully. "You a senior?"

"Junior," I replied.

"Have you met anybody? Kids, I mean."

"Just you," I said, laughing.

He laughed, too. A silent laugh that sounded more like coughing.

"Then I guess I should show you around or something," he said, suddenly shy.

He should be on TV, I thought. He's so great-looking!

"I could give you a bike tour of Shocklin Falls," he offered, motioning to his bike. "That'll take a minute or two," he joked.

"Well, I've sort of had the bike tour," I said.

And instantly regretted it.

Why did I say that? I scolded myself. He was offering to ride around with me, and I told him no.

What a jerk I am!

I could feel my face redden again.

Jonathan stared at me thoughtfully. "I'll introduce you to some Shocklin kids," he said.

"Great!" I gushed. "I mean . . ."

He turned his gaze toward the woods, as if he saw something. "I have this friend," he started. "He's my best buddy. I mean, he's a total dork, but he's my best buddy. Actually, he's a wild man. You'll like him."

"Great," I repeated, starting to stammer again. Was he planning to fix me up with this wild-man friend?

"His name is Caleb," Jonathan continued, still staring toward the woods. "Caleb Dorsey." He snickered, as if remembering something funny about Caleb.

"Caleb's parents have to work every Friday night," Jonathan continued. "So we all get together at Caleb's and have like a party. You know. Every Friday. It's great. It gets pretty wild sometimes."

"Sounds great," I said.

Why couldn't I think of some other word? I scolded myself. How many times in one conversation can a person use the word *great*?

He must think I'm a real jerk.

"So would you like to go with me Friday night? To Caleb's, I mean?" His green eyes seemed to light up as he stared at me expectantly.

"You mean, like a date?" I asked.

Annie — shape up! I ordered myself. *It's not like you've never been on a date before. You were pretty popular back in Middletown.*

"Yeah," Jonathan said, grinning. "Like a date."

"Sure," I said. "Great!"

Great?

Did I really say it again?

"Great," he repeated softly. He kicked at the dirt with his sneaker and glanced at the falls. "I've got to go."

"Me, too," I said.

The sun dipped behind a wide white cloud. The air grew chillier. Shadows slid along the ground.

We made our way across the dirt to get our bikes.

I was feeling really good.

It was only my third day in Shocklin Falls. And the first boy I'd met, a really great-looking guy, had asked me out.

Not a bad start, I thought.

Not bad at all.

Jonathan picked up his bike by the handle-bars and walked it over to me. Then we headed around to the other side of the big rocks where I had left mine.

To my surprise, the bike was standing up, tilted against a rock.

I remembered just letting it fall when I went running over to Jonathan, thinking he was going to jump.

Strange, I thought.

And then I gasped loudly. "Whoa!"

I hurried over to the bike and bent low to examine it.

"Hey — what's going on?" I cried, my heart pounding in my chest.

Both tires had been slashed to ribbons.

Chapter 3

"I don't believe this," I muttered.

I ran one hand over the cut tire. A chunk of rubber fell off in my hand.

"Who — " I started, but the words caught in my throat.

I was crouched down, staring in total disbelief at the slashed tires on Kenny's bike. Jonathan was standing right behind me, his shadow falling over me.

"I don't get it," he said quietly. "There's no one else up here."

I gazed up at him. His eyes were narrowed on the woods, as if searching for someone there. I followed his glance. The trees were mostly bare. It would be easy to see someone running away.

The woods were empty.

I shuddered. I suddenly felt cold all over.

"Kenny's going to kill me," I whispered, climbing to my feet.

"Who's Kenny?" Jonathan asked, still searching the woods.

"My little brother. It's his bike."

Jonathan scowled. "I'll help you walk it home," he said glumly, avoiding my eyes.

"That's okay," I said. "I can — "

"No." He grabbed the handlebars of Kenny's bike. "Take my bike. I'll walk this one," he snapped. He suddenly sounded very angry.

I obediently took his bike. We began to walk side by side along the bike path.

"This is so dumb," I said. "Why would someone do this to me?"

Jonathan didn't answer.

"I mean, who would climb all the way up to the top of the falls just to wreck some stranger's bike?" I continued, my voice trembling.

Jonathan still didn't reply.

His angry expression startled me into silence.

Why was *he* so angry? It wasn't *his* bike!

His mood had changed so quickly, it frightened me.

We followed the path as it curved down through the woods. The sun remained behind clouds. The woods were shadowy now, shadowy and cold. As if spring had left and winter had returned.

It seemed to take forever to get down to the street.

I felt so awkward. I wanted to talk, to say something. Anything. But Jonathan kept his eyes lowered to the ground, his jaw clenched. I could see the veins throbbing angrily at his temples.

So I remained silent, too.

I just didn't get it. He volunteered to walk me home, after all. I wasn't *forcing* him.

Was he angry at me?

I was totally confused. It didn't make any sense.

The ground leveled out when we reached Main Street. The sun reappeared, but it was nearly evening and the air remained cool.

"I live on Edgevale," I said softly.

"Okay," Jonathan replied, his expression a blank.

Then we heard a sound behind us. A girl's voice calling.

We both stopped and turned around.

A girl rode up on a sleek red bike. "Jonathan!" she called, flashing him a warm smile.

She had curly red hair, which cascaded down her shoulders like a waterfall, and a face full of freckles. She wasn't exactly pretty. Her blue-gray eyes were kind of close together, and she had a short stub of a nose. I guess you'd call her "cute."

She was wearing black Lycra leggings and an oversized blue-and-white Shocklin High T-shirt with a big S on the front.

"Ruby!" Jonathan cried. Even though she was smiling at him so warmly, he didn't exactly seem pleased to see her.

"Hi," she said breathlessly, lowering her sneakers to the road. She glanced at me, then quickly returned her smile to Jonathan. "What's happening?"

"Bike trouble," Jonathan replied curtly.

Ruby giggled for some reason.

"This is Annie," Jonathan told her. "Annie . . . uh . . ."

"Kiernan," I said. "Annie Kiernan. And that's my bike." I pointed to the bike Jonathan was walking. "I mean, it's my brother's."

"I'm Ruby Bonds," she said and, tossing her red hair behind her shoulders, quickly turned her attention back to Jonathan. I wasn't sure she had even looked at me.

"Ruby, where are you coming from?" Jonathan asked. "Up at the falls?"

"Huh-uh." Her smile faded as she shook her head. She blushed. "No way. I've just been riding around. I've been cooped up all day helping my mom with spring-cleaning. So I wanted to get a little exercise."

"You see Dawn today?" Jonathan asked.

"No. I'm going over there tonight," Ruby told him. "Just to hang out."

"Annie just moved here," Jonathan said, suddenly remembering I was still there.

"Oh," Ruby replied, not terribly interested. But then she turned, narrowing her eyes to check me out. "What happened to your bike?" she asked.

"Somebody cut the tires," I told her. "I really can't believe it."

Ruby glanced dryly at Jonathan. "I believe it," she muttered under her breath. She flashed Jonathan a look I couldn't interpret.

Something was going on between the two of them, but I couldn't figure out what.

Was Ruby the person Jonathan was waiting to meet up at the falls? If she was, wouldn't he ask her why she didn't show up?

I decided he had to be waiting for someone else.

I had the feeling that Jonathan didn't like Ruby. She kept smiling at him, but I couldn't tell how she felt about him.

"I've got to go," Ruby said suddenly. She fiddled with the gear control on her handlebars. Then she turned to me. "Watch out for Jonathan," she said through gritted teeth. "Really. He's dangerous. A real dangerous guy."

"Ruby — !" Jonathan started to protest.

But Ruby called out, "Later!" and sped off, standing on her pedals and quickly disappearing around the corner.

"She's weird," Jonathan said. "She was kidding about me. You know? Ruby and I are old pals."

I saw that Jonathan was staring at me intently, studying my reaction to what Ruby had said.

"Yeah. I could tell she was joking," I said.

But I wasn't so sure.

She hadn't *looked* as if she were joking. She had looked very serious.

Was she really warning me to stay away from Jonathan?

Did she mean that he *really* was dangerous?

What a crazy idea.

I glanced once again at Jonathan. He looked perfectly okay to me.

Better than okay!

With those wild green eyes and that dark, tanned skin, he reminded me suddenly of a tiger.

Tigers are dangerous, I warned myself.

I don't care, I thought.

A short while later, we were standing at the

foot of my driveway. We traded bikes. "Thanks," I said, "for walking me home."

"That's okay. Sorry about your bike."

"You want to come in or something?" I offered.

He shook his head. "I've got to get home. See you in school Monday."

"Yeah. Great," I said. And then I added, "Nice meeting you." It sounded really stupid and phony.

He ignored it. "And don't forget Friday night," he said, climbing onto his bike.

"I won't. I'm looking forward to it."

That's for sure!

I watched him ride away, those long legs pedaling quickly, easily.

I turned and started to drag Kenny's bike up the driveway. But then I stopped.

Who was that at the corner?

Someone was waiting under the shadows of a tall hedge. Someone on a bike, keeping close to the hedge. Waiting for Jonathan.

I stepped back toward the street, squinting hard to see who it was.

Ruby!

She was waiting for him at the corner. She pedaled away from the hedge, out of the shadows, as he came near.

They talked for a moment, close together, side by side on their bikes.

And then I watched them ride off together.

What's going on here? I wondered.

What exactly is going on?

Chapter 4

Caleb Dorsey was the kind of guy who thought it was hilarious to smash soda cans against his forehead and burp real loud.

He had long, stringy brown hair that looked as if it hadn't been washed in a month. I spotted a thin gold earring in one ear. His face seemed to be locked in a wide grin, his dark eyes crinkled in laughter. I couldn't imagine a serious expression on his face.

Caleb was tall and lanky and never seemed to stand still. He was very fidgety, very hyper. He bounced around his small, crowded living room, wearing a T-shirt that was too small for him and baggy, faded jeans with enormous holes at the knees, jiggling his shoulders, slapping high fives, shouting and laughing.

At first I couldn't imagine Caleb and Jonathan being best friends. But after a few hours, I realized that Caleb brought out a lighter side of Jonathan. Around Caleb, Jonathan loosened up and became funny, and wild, and loud. Almost as if he were competing with his friend.

I was pretty nervous, being the outsider, the new kid. So I spent a lot of time on the outskirts of the crowd, studying the others.

It was Friday night. Jonathan had picked me up in a brand-new, silver Volvo station wagon and had driven us to Caleb's small box of a house for the usual Friday night blowout.

Jonathan seemed pretty relaxed, and I pretended to be. But my stomach was knotted, and my hands were cold as ice. I mean, it was our first date, and here we were going to a party where he knew everyone and I didn't know a soul.

I had spent at least an hour up in my room puzzling over what to wear. I'd finally ended up in a silky white, long-sleeved top and a short, black Betsey Johnson skirt over black tights.

As we walked in through the kitchen door, I saw that most of the girls were in jeans, but I didn't care.

Even though it was a cool night out, the house was steamy hot. I spotted about twenty kids, maybe more, jammed into the small living room and spilling into a narrow front hallway.

The music was so loud, the windows rattled.

Everyone had to shout to be heard over the noise.

Some couples were dancing near the living room door. A big group of kids hung out in the center of the living room, laughing and talking. Two couples were pressed together on the narrow stairway leading upstairs, making out, one couple on the bottom step, the other nearly hidden in darkness halfway up the stairs.

Most kids were carrying around cans of soda, but I saw several holding cans of beer. Even though they were away at work, Caleb's parents must know about his Friday night parties, I thought. But I wondered if they knew about the beer.

Holding my hand loosely, Jonathan led me into the crowded living room. Over the voices and music, I distinctly heard someone ask, "Is that Jonathan's new girlfriend?" I turned, but I didn't see who said it.

Caleb came bouncing over, grinning. His grin didn't fade as he checked me out. Jonathan introduced us, shoving Caleb back a foot or two.

"Watch out for this jerk," Caleb warned me, shoving Jonathan back. "He doesn't look it, but he's an animal."

I laughed. But it flashed in my mind that

Caleb was the second person to tell me to watch out for Jonathan.

"You're not animal. You're vegetable," Jonathan told Caleb.

"You're not even vegetable," Caleb replied. "You're sponge."

"If I'm a sponge, *you're* the stuff you have to wipe up with a sponge!" Jonathan exclaimed.

The two of them collapsed, laughing.

Shaking his head, Jonathan said something to me, but I couldn't hear him over the music.

Caleb moved close to me and wrapped a heavy arm around my shoulder. "Don't pay attention to Jonathan and me," he said, bringing his face close to mine. I smelled beer on his breath. "We're both jerks."

"And proud of it!" Jonathan declared, grinning. He raked a hand back through his flattop as his eyes searched the room. "Where's Dawn?" he asked Caleb.

Caleb shrugged and slapped a short kid hard on the back, making him spill his soda on the carpet. The kid didn't even turn around, just kept talking to two other guys.

"Here I am," a girl's voice called from behind me.

I turned to see a tall, dramatic-looking girl with piles of long, curly black hair, big, dark eyes, and dark, lipsticked lips. Despite her black hair and dark features, she had very pale, creamy white skin. She wore short, bright blue shorts over a gray Lycra catsuit. Very sexy.

"Caleb, can't you turn the music down?" she demanded, stepping past me.

"No way." He gave her a goofy grin.

"I can't hear myself think," she shouted.

"Who wants to think?" was Caleb's reply.

"Caleb hates new experiences," Jonathan commented dryly. He turned to me. "Annie, this is Dawn Pedderson."

"Hi," Dawn shouted over the music. "You're here with *him*?" She pointed to Jonathan and made a face.

I nodded.

"You must be new here," Dawn teased. She tossed her hair back over her shoulder. She seemed to play with her hair a lot, tugging at it, tangling it around her hand, then pushing it off her face.

"Yeah," I said. "I just moved here."

I turned to Jonathan, but he and Caleb had disappeared somewhere.

I felt abandoned.

As I looked for him, my eyes stopped on the couple making out at the bottom of the stairs. I couldn't see her face, but I recognized the girl's red hair.

"Ruby!" I declared.

"Have you met Ruby?" Dawn asked, stepping close beside me and following my gaze.

"Yeah," I said, staring. "Who's the guy?"

"I don't recognize him," Dawn replied. "I don't think he goes to Shocklin." She snickered. "Ruby probably doesn't know his name, either."

I laughed. I liked Dawn's nasty sense of humor.

"Some people do aerobics. Ruby does guys," Dawn said. And then she turned her eyes to me and her expression grew more intense. "She has a thing for Jonathan, too. Did you know that?"

"A thing?" I asked. I wasn't sure I'd heard right. It was so noisy.

I couldn't hear what Dawn said next.

The two of us found ourselves wandering back toward the kitchen, away from the stereo speakers and the crowd. The kitchen was empty. Someone had spilled a bag of potato chips across the yellow Formica counter.

There was a stack of dirty dishes in the sink. I stepped around a brown puddle of Coke on the linoleum floor.

Dawn and I leaned against the counter, chatting and absently picking up the spilled potato chips and eating them as we talked. She was nearly a foot taller than me. She kept complaining that she was overweight, but in my opinion, she was just well-built. I looked like a short little beanpole next to her.

I told her about moving from Ohio, how hard it was to leave my friends behind, to start at a new school so late in the school year.

We both jumped when we heard a loud crash from the living room. "Typical," Dawn said, rolling her eyes. "I can't believe Caleb's parents put up with this."

"Caleb's a riot," I said, reaching for another potato chip. "He's so funny!"

"Funny-looking," Dawn muttered. "Caleb and I have been going together for about six months. Off and on."

I gazed at her in surprise. I couldn't imagine Caleb and Dawn as a couple. "Off and on?" I asked.

"Sometimes I get sick of him," she admitted, glancing to the kitchen doorway. "I mean, he's just never serious. That can be a lot of fun for a while. But sometimes I just want to shake him and say, 'Knock it off. Stop with the jokes. Be serious!' He can be a real pain. I mean, he's always getting into trouble at school. Always . . ." She stopped.

"Yeah?" I urged.

She shrugged. "He's okay, I guess. He makes me laugh. And once you really get to know him, he's a good guy." She sighed and tapped a potato chip against the counter until it crumbled. Then she raised her eyes to mine.

"There's something you should know about Jonathan," she said, lowering her voice, her expression turning solemn.

"Huh? About Jonathan?"

"Yeah. He's been through a bad time. He — "

She didn't get to finish her sentence. Caleb burst into the room and grabbed her arm. "Come on, Dawn — we're all going now."

She pulled out of his grasp. "Huh? Going where?"

"To Sportsworld," he replied, tugging her again. He turned to me. "You, too. Come on."

"What's Sportsworld?" I asked.

"Batting cages," Dawn answered, making a face. "You know. One of those places with basketball courts, and Ping-Pong tables, and — "

"You can watch me outslug Jonathan," Caleb said, grinning. "We made a little bet." He put his hands together and bent his knees in a ridiculously exaggerated batting stance. Then he swung all the way around, toppling into the kitchen counter.

"Caleb, how are you going to outslug Jonathan? You can't outslug *me*!" Dawn declared, shaking her head.

"You kidding?" He cried, acting as if his feelings were hurt. "You swing like a *girl*!"

"Cute," Dawn muttered. "That's real cute." She gave him a hard, playful shove, then followed him to the living room.

I followed Dawn, then stopped in the hallway. Across the room, I saw Ruby standing with Jonathan. She had a hand on his cheek. They were talking with their faces close together.

I think he saw me because he pulled Ruby's hand away from his face and stepped away from her. I made my way across the room, pushing past a circle of kids who were laughing uproariously about something.

"Hey, I lost you," he said as I approached, flashing me a smile. "You remember Ruby?"

I said hi to Ruby, and she nodded. "You get your bike fixed?" she asked, shouting over the laughter across from us.

"It wasn't my bike," I told her. "It was my brother's."

She didn't react. I thought maybe she didn't hear me.

Caleb grabbed my shoulder. "Come on, guys. Let's go!"

Jonathan flashed me a guilty smile. "Is it okay with you? I sort of made a bet with Caleb."

"Sure," I said. "Sounds like fun."

A few seconds later, about ten of us had piled into two cars, and we were roaring past town toward Sportsworld. I sat beside Jonathan in the front of the station wagon, with four kids I didn't know in the back.

Jonathan drove like a madman. He had the radio cranked up as loud as it would go, and he kept careening deliberately from side to side on the road, going at least seventy-five the whole way.

"Jonathan — !" I shouted when he bumped over the curb into someone's yard. "Stop it!"

His eyes were wild with excitement, and his grin just grew wider. "I can handle it," he shouted.

He turned the wheel wildly, and the car squealed back into the street.

"Do you always drive like this?" I asked.

He stared into the windshield, a strange grin fixed on his face, looking almost as if he were hypnotized.

"Jonathan — ?"

I was so relieved when we finally reached Sportsworld, a brightly lit, indoor–outdoor sports arena more than a block long. Jonathan turned into the parking lot, the tires squealing, and came to an abrupt, bone-jarring stop. I pushed open my car door and practically leapt out, grateful to be in one piece.

To my surprise, Caleb and his group were already going inside. Caleb must be an even crazier driver than Jonathan, I realized.

I slammed the car door and jogged after Jonathan, who was already moving across the parking lot toward the entrance. "Whew! What a ride!" I cried breathlessly. "That was scary, Jonathan."

He stopped and turned to me. His smile faded. Those amazing green eyes seemed to burn into mine. "Sometimes I just feel wild," he said. "Like, out of control. You know."

He stood staring at me, hands at his waist, as if waiting for me to reply. But I didn't know what to say. His driving had really frightened me. He *did* seem out of control.

His expression softened. He smiled. "Just kidding," he said. His green eyes seemed to twinkle under the parking lot lights. He was so handsome! "Come on. Let's go hit some baseballs."

We started jogging across the parking lot to catch up to the others.

I saw Dawn up ahead of us, and I suddenly remembered what she had started to tell me in the kitchen: "There's something you should know about Jonathan."

What had she started to tell me?

Did it have something to do with the way he drove, with his need to get "out of control"?

He seemed to have such drastic mood changes.

Was that what Dawn wanted to warn me about?

The batting cages were outdoors, in back of the building, under daylight-bright lights. I could see a row of eight or ten of them, long canvas-and-wire mesh cages with pitching machines near the far end.

The place was incredibly crowded. Jammed with teenagers and a lot of loud, young, working people. We had to wait for a batting cage. I kept close to Jonathan, peering through the mesh into the cages, watching helmeted batters take their swings against ninety m.p.h. pitches.

"Look at that guy. He's swinging an hour late on every pitch," Jonathan said, snickering.

It was a chilly night. It felt more like winter than spring. I shivered. I wished I'd worn a sweatshirt or something.

Jonathan was shouting encouragement to the guy in the batting cage. He seemed to be enjoying himself. I wondered if he liked me.

Suddenly, I heard a loud, rattling sound above our heads. Startled, I looked up to see Caleb clinging to the side of the cage, ten or twenty feet above the ground. He was holding onto the mesh with one hand, making chimpanzee gestures with his other hand.

"Oh, man!" Jonathan cried, and then he totally cracked up.

"Get down!" a man cried from somewhere behind us.

"Hey — that's dangerous!" someone else screamed.

"Me Tarzan!" Caleb shouted, climbing to the top of the cage.

"Caleb's so messed up!" Jonathan exclaimed gleefully. "He's crazy! He'll do *anything*!"

My eye caught Dawn, a few yards away. She didn't appear at all amused. In fact, her face was bright red, and she looked really embarrassed.

I saw two guys wearing dark blue pants and white shirts come hurrying over. They must work here, I realized.

"Hey — get down!" one of them waved furiously at Caleb.

"What are you doing?" the other one shouted.

Caleb ignored the two men. "Hey, Jonathan — join me?" he called down. "You get a better view up here!"

"Do you *believe* him?" Jonathan asked me, still laughing.

"Come on, man," Caleb called down to Jonathan. "You chicken?"

Jonathan stared up at his friend.

"Come on up, wimp!" Caleb called down.

The smile faded from Jonathan's face.

I shuddered.

Jonathan had the strangest expression on his face. Fear mixed with anger. His entire body went rigid. He stared up at Caleb without moving.

What is wrong? I wondered.

What is Jonathan thinking about?

Why does he suddenly look so strange, so frightening?

"Hey — chicken face!" Caleb called down, waving his free hand, clinging to the wire mesh with the other. "Chicken face!"

Jonathan glanced nervously at me. Then he started to call up to Caleb. But Jonathan's words choked in his throat, and his eyes widened with horror.

As Caleb motioned enthusiastically for Jonathan to climb up, his hand slipped away from the mesh.

He started to fall.

I watched Caleb plummet all the way down without realizing that the hideous scream I heard the whole time was coming from me.

Chapter 5

I was surrounded by screams and cries of horror.

Jonathan grabbed my shoulder.

Caleb landed easily on his hands and knees. He rolled over once. Twice. Then climbed to his feet, a goofy, triumphant grin on his face.

"Ta-*daa!*" he sang.

There were groans and loud sighs of relief. Excited voices rang out through the entire area.

The two grim-faced workers came up on either side of Caleb and grabbed his arms.

"Hey, what's the problem?" Caleb demanded. "I mean, what's the problem?"

Jonathan was still holding tight to my shoulder. I turned to him. He seemed somewhat dazed by the whole thing. "You okay?" I asked.

He shook his head. Seemed to snap out of it. "Yeah. I — I was just thinking about something else." Avoiding my eyes, he let go of my shoulder.

Caleb was arguing with the two workers, who wanted to throw him out. Dawn came up to me, toying nervously with a thick strand of black hair. "Read any good books lately?" she asked dryly.

"I — I really thought he was going to kill himself this time," Jonathan said.

"*This* time?" I asked.

"Yeah. He's done it before," Dawn told me.

"He does stuff like that all the time," Jonathan said, shaking his head. "He always lands on his feet."

"Or his head," Dawn said with surprising bitterness. "But it never knocks any sense into him."

The two men were leading Caleb out to the exit. I watched Dawn run to catch up with them. She seemed really angry and upset. Again I thought of what a strange couple Dawn and Caleb were. They were so different from each other. And she didn't even seem to like him that much.

Jonathan had picked a bat up from the bat rack at the side of the cage. He swung it hard once, as if hitting an imaginary pitch. "Looks like our competition is over," he said quietly. "Sorry."

"That's okay," I replied. I was shivering. It was a really cold night.

"Let's go," he said. He tossed the bat to the ground and headed toward the exit.

People were still talking and laughing about Caleb climbing on top of the batting cage. As I followed Jonathan out, I pictured again the strange expression on his face when Caleb had called for him to climb up, too.

Was it fear?

Was it anger?

Was it jealousy?

His green eyes had filled with such sadness. What had he been thinking of?

I realized I was probably reading too much into it. Jonathan was probably just afraid for Caleb's safety.

I do that a lot.

"You think too much." That's what my mom always tells me.

I over-analyze everything. I find dark meanings in things that have no meaning at all.

But why was I feeling so troubled as Jonathan and I made our way to his station wagon?

You're just nervous, Annie, I told myself. It's your first date with Jonathan, and you're not sure if he likes you or not.

And why should he like me?

I'd been so quiet all night. I felt like such an

outsider among all these kids who'd known each other forever.

He'll never ask me out again, I thought as I slid into the front seat of the car and pulled the door shut. The leather seat was ice-cold.

Jonathan started up the car. Two other couples had piled into the back. "Can you turn on some heat?" I asked, folding my arms around myself, trying to get warm.

"No problem," he said, reaching for the dials.

He drove home carefully, keeping below the speed limit. Everyone joked about Caleb and his climb. A boy in the back seat told a story about Caleb breaking into an indoor swimming pool and being caught swimming naked with a bunch of kids. A girl told a story about how Caleb was arrested one night breaking into his own house!

"He's been arrested twenty times!" another boy declared.

Everyone laughed except for Jonathan. "Caleb's not a criminal," Jonathan said earnestly. "I mean, he's never been convicted of anything. He always pleads *insanity*!"

Everyone laughed again, including Jonathan this time.

Laughing and joking, we dropped the other kids off.

I was feeling really good and had finally gotten warm by the time Jonathan pulled the station wagon up my driveway. He shifted into Park, but didn't shut off the engine.

The porch light was on, and the lights were on in my parents' bedroom upstairs. The clock on the dashboard read 11:24. Still pretty early.

I wondered if Jonathan was going to kiss me.

Gazing at him in the pale white light from the porch, I realized I wanted him to.

His eyes studied the green lights on the dashboard. I wondered what he was thinking.

Was he trying to decide whether or not to kiss me?

Was he nervous, too?

Was he thinking about me at all?

His expression was a total blank. I couldn't read it.

"Well, that's a typical night in Shocklin Falls," he said, turning toward me and smiling.

"I enjoyed it," I said, smiling back.

"Me, too," he said automatically.

Was he going to lean toward me and kiss me?

No.

"See you in school," he said.

"Yeah. Okay."

I gave him a few more seconds. But he kept both hands on the wheel. So I pushed open the door and climbed out.

The headlights rolled over the front of the house as I found my keys and pushed open the front door.

I felt disappointed.

I felt like a total jerk.

The front hallway and living room were dark.

Without bothering to turn on the lights, I hung my jacket in the front closet.

Then I started to make my way through the darkness to the stairs when someone leapt at me and two hands grabbed my shoulders from behind.

Chapter 6

Uttering a silent gasp, I stumbled forward into the banister.

I heard footsteps pad across the floor.

"Goggles!" I cried out in a choked whisper.

I clicked on the hall light. The stupid cat was standing at my feet, staring up at me.

"Goggles, how many times do I have to tell you not to scare me like that?" I asked, picking him up.

He purred excitedly.

I touched his nose to mine.

"Don't jump on me," I told him for the thousandth time. "I don't have nine lives like you do."

I hugged him close, rubbing my hand down his soft, white fur. "You don't understand a word I'm saying, do you, stupid?"

He purred contentedly as I stroked his back. Then he swiped at me with his paw, his way of telling me he'd had enough affection.

I set him down and he padded away.

Goggles has some bad habits. Jumping on people in the dark is one of his worst. But I love him just the same. He is so pretty with all that fluffy white fur and those big, serious blue eyes.

I had started up the stairs, thinking about Jonathan, when my mother's voice interrupted my thoughts. "Annie, is that you?"

Who *else* would it be?

"Yes, it's me," I called.

She appeared at the upstairs railing, her hair down, wearing a long pink flannel nightgown. "How was your date?"

"Fine."

I always give the same reply to that question. What does she expect — *details*?

"What did you do?" my mother asked, yawning loudly.

"Went to a party," I told her, starting the climb up the stairs. "Just a lot of kids hanging around."

"That's nice," she replied sleepily. "See you in the morning." She disappeared into her room.

A few minutes later, I was changed, in bed, thinking about Jonathan.

Once again, I heard the girl at Caleb's house

saying, "That's Jonathan's new girlfriend." I
wondered if I *was* Jonathan's new girlfriend.

I wondered if he'd ever ask me out again.

Before I realized it, I drifted into a sound
sleep. If I dreamed about Jonathan, I didn't
remember it in the morning.

I ran into Dawn in school on Monday morning. We talked for a while between classes. It
turned out we were in the same social studies
class.

I decided I really liked her. I hoped we could
become good friends.

During lunch period, I spotted Dawn at a
table in the corner of the cafeteria and I carried
my tray over to have lunch with her.

We talked about our social studies term papers. Dawn and the others in the class had a
real head start on me. They'd already been re-
searching their papers for three weeks. I knew
I'd be spending a lot of time in the library and
in the computer lab, typing up all my research,
trying to catch up with the others in the class.

Eventually, the conversation came around
to Jonathan.

"Where'd you meet him?" Dawn asked, taking a forkful of her tossed salad.

"Up at the falls," I replied.

She put down her fork. Her mouth dropped

open in surprise. "Huh? Where?"

"At the falls," I repeated, startled by her reaction.

She tossed a thick strand of black hair back over her shoulder and stared at me, studying my face as if trying to determine if I were telling the truth.

"I was bike riding," I said. "You know. Exploring. I followed the bike path up to the falls and — "

"I really can't believe Jonathan would go up there," Dawn interrupted, still staring at me intently. She picked up her fork and started tapping it nervously against the cafeteria tray.

"What's wrong, Dawn?" I asked.

Her dark eyes narrowed. "Are we talking about the same falls?"

"Is there more than one?" I asked innocently.

"No." She shook her head. "I just can't believe Jonathan would ever go up there again. I mean, after what happened."

I set down my slice of pizza. A sliver of cheese stuck to my thumb. I chewed it off. "Did something bad happen up there?" I asked. "To Jonathan?"

Dawn nodded. "Yeah. A few months ago. Last January."

She stopped, then started again. "I guess I

might as well tell you about it. I mean, everyone knows. It's not like a secret or anything.
That's for sure."

"What?" I cried impatiently. "What? What?
Stop being so mysterious. You're driving me
crazy!"

"I don't think you'll like it once you hear it,"
Dawn replied softly.

"*What's* driving you crazy?" demanded a
voice behind us.

I turned to see Ruby standing right behind
me, a loaded-up lunch tray in her hands. She
set the tray down beside me, across from
Dawn, and sat down. "You both look so serious," she said, moving the plates around on her
tray. "What are you talking about? Your hair?"

"Our social studies term papers," Dawn answered quickly, casting me a quick glance that
told me not to contradict with the truth.

Ruby brushed her red hair back over the
shoulder of her green Gap T-shirt and concentrated on pushing the straw into her juice box.
"We don't have term papers in Curtis's class,"
she told them. "We have a killer essay test
instead."

"I think I'd rather have the test," I said,
taking a bite of the small square of pizza. "I'm
getting such a late start."

"You wouldn't want *this* essay test," Ruby

insisted, picking up a hamburger, watching the grease drizzle from the bun. "It has real easy, specific questions, like, 'Compare and contrast everything on earth.' "

Dawn and I laughed appreciatively. That was a pretty good essay question.

We chatted about teachers and classes. All the while I was dying to hear what Dawn had started to tell me about Jonathan. But it was obvious Dawn didn't want to talk about it while Ruby was around.

What could it be? I wondered, my mind spinning with wild ideas.

Why was Dawn so surprised that Jonathan was up at the falls?

What happened up there?

We were nearly finished with our lunches when I felt a tap on my shoulder. I looked up to find Jonathan smiling down at me. He was wearing a pale blue sweater over dark, straight-legged jeans. He looked really great.

"Hi!" I cried, unable to hide my surprise. I'd looked for him all day, but hadn't seen him.

"How's it going?" he asked, glancing quickly at Dawn, then returning his attention to me. He pointed to my tray. "You like cardboard pizza?"

"It's my favorite," I replied. "It's going okay, I guess. I keep getting lost. This school is so much bigger than my old school."

"Have you seen Caleb?" Jonathan asked Dawn.

She made a face. "He's doing lunchtime detention."

Jonathan laughed. "What for?"

Dawn rolled her eyes. "He said a rude word to Mrs. Kelman."

"Caleb only knows rude words," Jonathan said, snickering. "Annie, did you get your new bike?"

I nodded. "I got a used one. The new ones were too expensive. It's excellent, though. Twenty-one speed."

Jonathan leaned close. "Great. Want to go riding Saturday afternoon?"

I had promised my dad I'd help him unpack some of the cartons in the garage, but I knew I could get out of it. "Yeah. Great," I said. "Come pick me up, okay?"

"Okay." Jonathan disappeared as quickly as he had appeared.

I felt really happy. Maybe Jonathan *didn't* think I was a total drip. Maybe he *did* like me.

My smile faded when I caught Ruby's expression. She was biting her lower lip, her features in a tight frown. She was suddenly pale white, sickly white.

"Ruby — are you feeling okay?" I blurted out.

"No, not really," she replied weakly. She let the rest of her hamburger drop to the tray and scooted her chair back. "I think this food made me sick or something."

"Can I help you — ?" I started. But she jumped to her feet and hurried out of the lunch room without looking back.

"Think we should go with her?" I asked Dawn.

Dawn shook her head. "She'll be okay." She'd been toying with her salad the whole time, but had hardly eaten a bite.

"Aren't you starving?" I asked.

Dawn nodded. "Yeah. But I've got to lose weight. I hate having a boyfriend who's skinnier than I am."

"I think you're just about perfect," I blurted out, and then was immediately embarrassed that I'd said it. But it was true. I'd give anything to look like Dawn instead of having this short, little-boyish figure.

Dawn picked up her tray and climbed to her feet. "Ready?"

I nodded. "Yeah. But you've got to finish what you were telling me. About Jonathan."

Her expression turned serious. "Okay, Annie. I'll tell you," she said softly. "But it may change everything. Really."

"I don't understand," I said. "Change what?"

"The way you feel about Jonathan, for one thing," Dawn replied. "You see, it's about the girl who died. Have you heard about it?"

Died?

The word stuck in my mind. It stayed there, echoing as if it would never fade away.

Died?

What girl?

We deposited our trays on the dirty-tray counter. The floor seemed to tilt beneath my feet. The fluorescent lights above us appeared to flash like bright explosions.

Maybe I *don't* want to hear this, I thought, shutting my eyes till the flashing stopped.

"No. I haven't heard about it," I told Dawn, my voice shaky.

I followed her out of the lunch room. She led us up the stairs and down the hall that led to the principal's office in the front of the building.

The hall was crowded and noisy, filled with kids who had finished their lunch and were messing around, waiting for the fifth-period bell to ring.

I didn't pay any attention to them. I followed Dawn, wondering where she was leading us, what she was going to tell me. And as we walked, my stomach tightened with dread. My hands turned cold. My heart began to race.

"*It may change everything,*" Dawn had said.

Everything.

What could she be talking about?

We turned a corner. We were near the front entrance. The principal's office stood diagonally across from the big double doorways. And in the wall beside the office stood a large glass display case, the kind usually used for showing off sports trophies.

Dawn stopped in front of the display case. She pushed her thick black hair back behind her head with both hands and peered into my eyes. "This is the girl who died," she said, gesturing to the glass case. "She died up at the falls."

I swallowed hard and stared into the case.

It was empty except for a single photograph. A color enlargement of a school photo.

It was a photo of a pretty girl. She had all-American good looks. Bright blonde hair. Flashing blue eyes. High cheekbones like a model. A beautiful smile revealing perfect white teeth.

The photo was draped with black crepe.

Beneath the photo stood a small black tag. It read: 1978–1993.

I stared into the girl's eyes. They stared coldly back at me.

After a few seconds, I had to look away.

"She died?" I asked Dawn in a tight, shrill voice. "Who is she? I mean, who was she?"

"That's Louisa," Dawn answered softly. "Jonathan's girlfriend."

Chapter 7

I stared through the glass at the photo of Louisa.

I stared at those round blue eyes, at that perfect smile, at the honey-blonde hair, brushed casually back, so soft against her perfect skin.

The black crepe draped around the photo didn't belong.

She was so light, so pretty, so . . . happy.

I couldn't picture her wearing black.

She shouldn't be in this dark, heavy case, I thought. She shouldn't be here with her dates under her photo.

The display case was like a glass casket. I was staring into Louisa's casket.

Staring at her smiling face, her pretty blue eyes.

I turned away with a violent shudder. I felt that I was somehow invading her privacy.

"She was Jonathan's girlfriend?" I asked Dawn.

Dawn nodded.

I wanted to ask more. A hundred questions flooded my mind. I wanted to know everything about her. I wanted to know what she was like. And I wanted to know how she died.

And why did Dawn say it would change my idea of Jonathan?

But the fifth-period bell rang right over our heads. The hall rang out with kids stampeding noisily to class.

Dawn gave me a quick wave and hurried away, leaving me standing there.

Standing there with Louisa.

My eyes locked on Louisa's once again. And as I stared, the voices and laughter echoing down the hall faded away.

Louisa and I were alone.

What is your story, Louisa? I asked silently. What happened to you up at the falls?

She stared back at me through the glass.

1978–1993.

The dates seemed to shimmer and then blur.

Was that *sadness* I detected deep in those blue eyes? Sadness behind the posed smile?

I had to force myself to turn away.

To my surprise, the hall was nearly empty.

The second bell was about to ring, and I hadn't even collected my books.

How long had I been standing there?

I knew I had to talk to Dawn, had to find out the answers to all my questions. Avoiding the display case, I jogged past it and headed to my locker.

I'll call Dawn later, I decided.

I'll make her tell me everything.

The afternoon seemed to drag on for days. I was very distracted. I don't think I heard a word anyone said.

After school, I spent a couple of long, dreary hours in the computer lab, typing my social studies research onto a disk. Normally, I enjoy doing research. I like digging around in old books for facts and information. It's sort of like being an archaeologist.

But I had joined the class so late, and I was so far behind everyone else, I felt really pressured. Shocklin High seemed a lot more intense than my old school. Also, I wasn't used to the kind of computers they had in the computer lab, so I kept making mistakes.

That night, struggling to concentrate on my math homework, I found myself still thinking about Louisa, still eager to unravel the mystery about her. I kept calling Dawn all evening. At first, there was no answer. And then the line was busy for hours.

So frustrating!

I didn't get to talk to Dawn about Louisa until lunch period the next day. I forced Dawn to gulp down her lunch. (She was only having a salad anyway.) And then I dragged her to the display case in front of the building.

"You have to tell me the whole story," I insisted, staring at the photograph, finding myself searching once again for the sadness in Louisa's eyes. "What happened to her?"

Dawn hesitated. She leaned against the tile wall, toying thoughtfully with a thick strand of black hair, wrapping it and unwrapping it around her finger. "You sure you want to know?"

"Yeah. I'm sure," I replied impatiently. "Tell me what happened."

"No one really knows," Dawn said, still fingering her hair. "I mean, no one knows for sure."

I groaned. "Start at the beginning," I urged.

Dawn waited for a group of cheerleaders to pass. They were in their blue-and-white uniforms, laughing and playfully shoving each other into the walls.

When they had turned the corner, Dawn let

go of her hair and took a step closer to me. "It happened last January. It was a really warm day for January. Louisa and Jonathan went bike riding up to the falls. Somehow, Louisa and her bike went over the falls. And she died."

I gasped and shut my eyes. "Over the falls?"

I tried not to picture it. It was so horrible.

The falls were so steep. The water crashed straight down. Down onto those jagged black rocks.

"Over the falls," Dawn repeated softly.

"But, Jonathan — " I started. I didn't really know what I wanted to say.

"Jonathan told everyone he had left Louisa for a minute or two," Dawn continued, staring into the display case, her hands knotted into tight fists at her sides. "Jonathan said he saw someone. Back on the bike path. Or, he thought he saw someone. Anyway," Dawn sighed, "he went to see who it was. And when he came back . . ."

She didn't finish her sentence.

I swallowed hard, staring into the display case. Louisa's photo was just a blur of color to me now, all blues and pinks, surrounded by black.

"When he came back, Louisa was gone?" I managed to ask.

Dawn nodded. "Jonathan looked for her.

And then he saw her bike. Down below. All mangled. It had caught on the rocks."

"And Louisa?" I asked, my voice choked with the horror of it all.

"They dragged her body out downriver," Dawn said in a whisper. "Two days later. She was cut to pieces."

I gasped. "Someone had cut her?"

Dawn shook her head grimly. "The police said she'd been cut up by all the rocks."

I tried to focus on the photo in the display case, but it wouldn't come clear. I rested one hand against the wall to steady myself.

Such a horrible story.

And to think that I'd just been up at the falls. With Jonathan. I could picture it all so clearly. I could hear the roar of the falls in my ears. I could see the winding, dirt bike path and the woods behind it.

I could see the cliff edge over the falls.

I could see the black, pointed rocks in the river below.

I could see it all.

I turned to Dawn, who had folded her arms over her chest. "Why did she kill herself?" I managed to ask.

"What makes you think she killed herself?" Dawn asked with surprising emotion.

"Huh?" I gaped at her, trying to figure out what she was trying to tell me.

The principal, Mr. Thomasson, passed by, dabbing a wet handkerchief over a dark stain on his yellow necktie. He glanced up as he walked by us, nodded solemnly, and disappeared into his office, still working on the tie.

"I was Louisa's best friend," Dawn confided. "I thought she was perfectly happy." She sighed and lowered her eyes to the floor. Then she added, "I guess you never really know another person. Even a close friend. You never really know what's in their mind."

"But — "

"The police decided it was suicide," Dawn interrupted, still staring at her white sneakers. "In case you didn't already know it, Jonathan's parents are very rich. They got the police investigation to end very quickly."

Dawn's words stunned me. I raised my hands to my forehead and rubbed my throbbing temples.

"But no one suspected Jonathan — *did* they?" I asked, my voice choked with emotion.

"No, not really," Dawn replied reluctantly. She raised her eyes to mine. "But there were stories. You know. You know how rumors get started."

"What kinds of rumors?" I demanded.

"Just rumors," Dawn replied edgily. "Rumors that Jonathan and Louisa had had a big fight. That Jonathan wanted to break up with her and start going with someone else."

"Someone else?"

"Well . . . some kids saw his car parked in Ruby's driveway one night."

I stared hard at Dawn, trying to understand what she was saying, trying to read her mind, to figure out what she really believed had happened.

"Dawn, *you* don't think that Jonathan killed Louisa — do you?" I asked.

"No. Of course not," she replied quickly.

Too quickly.

She grabbed my arm and moved her face close to mine. "But I'd be careful, Annie," she whispered.

Careful?

What did she mean?

"I'd be really careful," she repeated in a low whisper, gripping my arm tightly.

"Dawn — ?"

"I've got to run," she said, letting go. "Later, okay?"

Before I could reply, she started jogging down the hall.

Be careful?

Her words remained in my mind.

What did she mean?

Did she mean to be careful of Jonathan?

Did she really think that Jonathan murdered Louisa? Pushed her over the falls? Then got his parents to hush it up with the police?

No. No way.

She *said* she didn't think that Jonathan had killed Louisa.

So why was Dawn warning me to be careful?

I shoved my hands into my jeans pockets and tried to stop from trembling. I wanted to walk away, to go to my locker, to go to my next class, to think about something else.

Anything else.

But Louisa wouldn't let me go.

Her black-draped photo beckoned to me, called me, pulled me in. I stood there staring through the glass at her.

Dawn had told me the whole story.

But she hadn't really told me any of it.

There is a story behind the story, isn't there, Louisa? I asked silently.

There are secrets you haven't revealed.

Secrets you may never reveal.

I stood there in the brightly lit hallway, hands shoved into my pockets, and stared at the photo as if searching the pretty face for the answers it hid.

I don't know how long I stared at it.

And I don't know how long it took me to realize that someone else had joined me. Someone else was standing right beside me, so close that his shoulder pressed against mine.

I don't know how long it took me to realize he was staring intently at me as I stared at Louisa.

"She didn't kill herself," he said.

Chapter 8

"What did you say?" I cried, startled.

I took a step away from him and studied his face. He wore round glasses with thin gold frames. He was short, shorter than me, and thin like a pencil. He had a lean face, with intense brown eyes, exaggerated by the eyeglasses. His brown hair stood straight up in a short flattop.

Taking another step back, I saw that he was wearing a green-and-black-striped polo shirt over baggy brown chinos.

He flashed me a nervous smile and blinked two or three times behind his glasses.

"Hi," he said shyly. "You were in the computer lab after school yesterday, right?" He had a surprisingly deep voice. He kept blinking nervously and shifting his books as he talked.

"Yeah," I replied.

"I was there, too. Did you see me?"

I shook my head and smiled at him. "I was concentrating so hard on keyboarding my research, I didn't see anybody," I confessed.

His narrow face fell in disappointment.

"My name is Ryan," he said shyly.

"Hi," I said. "Is that your first name or last?"

"I have two last names," he replied, a smile slowly spreading across his face. "I mean, both my names *could* be last names. Ryan is my first name. Ryan Baker."

I laughed. "Do you have a last name for a middle name?"

"No," he replied seriously. "I don't have a middle name. Just two last names."

"I'm Annie Kiernan," I told him.

"I know," he blurted out, then blushed. "I mean, I heard someone say your name. You just started here, right?"

"Right," I said. I glanced up at the clock outside the principal's office. The bell was going to ring any second.

He cleared his throat nervously and turned his gaze to Louisa's picture. "She was a really good friend of mine," he confided, his face completely expressionless. "I mean, we were *really* good friends."

"Yeah?" I didn't know what to say.

"We didn't go out or anything," Ryan continued, staring hard into the display case. "We were just really good friends. In fact . . ." He hesitated. He changed his mind about what he was going to say.

"What a terrible thing," I muttered awkwardly.

Something about Ryan made me feel very awkward and uncomfortable. I guess it was his nervousness.

"You've heard the whole story?" he asked, staring at Louisa.

"Yeah. Most of it," I replied.

"Well, she didn't kill herself!" he cried with surprising vehemence.

That's what I'd *thought* he'd said before.
She didn't kill herself.

"How do you know?" I blurted out, taking another step away from him.

"I know it," he snapped. He blushed again.

The bell rang, startling us both.

I hesitated. He didn't move. "Guess we should get to class," I said, eager to get away from him.

He nodded, still not moving. "Are you busy Saturday, Annie? Would you like to go to a movie or something?"

His question caught me by surprise. My mouth dropped open. I gaped at him as if I didn't understand what he was asking. I must have looked like a total jerk.

Why did Ryan make me feel so awkward?

"I guess you're probably busy," he muttered unhappily. "Well, some other time, maybe."

I remembered that I *did* have a date with Jonathan on Saturday, for the afternoon, at least.

"Yeah. Some other time," I said, feeling foolish. "Nice meeting you, Ryan."

He mumbled something, avoiding my eyes, and hurried away. I watched him disappear around the corner.

"Strange dude," I said aloud.

Then, taking one last glance at Louisa's photo, I turned away and hurried to class.

The afternoon was pretty much of a disaster.

I had done the wrong pages in the math workbook, and Mr. Woolrich insisted on making fun of me in front of the entire class.

Real sensitive guy, Mr. Woolrich.

And then I was trying to drink from the water fountain next to the gym, and the water went down the wrong pipe and, in front of a big crowd, some boy I'd never seen before started slapping my back to help me stop choking.

Of course it didn't help. And I was totally mortified.

I was pretty well wrecked by the time I got

up to the computer lab after school. I probably should have just gone home and vegged out with some MTV for the rest of the afternoon. But I still had several pages of research to type into the computer.

The computer lab was empty except for a couple of girls typing furiously away in the back. I looked for Ryan and was relieved to see that he wasn't there.

Just thinking about him made me uncomfortable.

Maybe I'm prejudiced against guys who are shorter than I am, I thought.

No. That wasn't the reason he made me feel awkward. It was just that he was so nervous and awkward himself.

And he was saying such revealing, frightening things to me, a total stranger.

"Louisa didn't kill herself."

Why did he say that to me? Was he deliberately trying to scare me or something?

I shook my head hard as if trying to shake Ryan out of my mind. Then I found my disk in the file and inserted it in the computer I had used before in the front row.

I booted the disk, located my file, and called it up.

The computer whirred, and the screen went black.

"Hey, wait!" I cried aloud.

Where were all the notes I had typed in yesterday?

I must have done something wrong. They must be here. They've *got* to be here.

"I *hate* these stupid computers," I muttered under my breath.

I turned off the machine and started again. I called up my file.

Again, the computer whirred obediently.

The name of my file appeared at the top.

But the rest of the screen was blank.

Completely blank.

My throat tightened. I suddenly felt sick.

"Where are you hiding my stuff?" I asked the computer.

I stared at the blank screen in angry disbelief.

My notes — all of my work — was gone.

Erased.

A heavy, sinking feeling in my stomach, I hit the keys, moving the screen down, page after page.

All erased. All a total blank.

Page after page after page.

"No!" I uttered a cry of total exasperation.

This can't be happening.

Wait.

There was something at the end of the file.

Two lines of type.

I was so upset, it took a while to focus on the words.

As I read the lines, the sinking feeling spread over my entire body, and I felt cold all over.

At the bottom of the screen were two short sentences:

STAY AWAY FROM JONATHAN.
IT COULD SAVE YOUR LIFE.

Chapter 9

It wasn't an accident, I realized.

All of my notes weren't erased by accident.
The computer didn't do it. A person did it.

Someone erased my work, then typed the
threatening message at the end.

"Who?" I cried, not realizing I was talking
aloud.

I turned and saw the two girls in the back
look up at me.

I clicked off the computer and, leaving the
disk in the machine, shoved my books into my
backpack and burst out of the room.

I was breathing hard. My temples throbbed.

I ran down the hall, my sneakers thudding
loudly on the hard floor, then down the stairs.

Who did that to me? I wondered.

All my hard work. And I was already so far
behind everyone else.

I felt like crying. But I forced myself not to.

Who did it?

I ran past the empty classrooms, past a janitor carrying two large gray wastebaskets, past rows of silent lockers.

I came to an abrupt halt in front of Louisa's display case.

Don't stop, I told myself.

But something kept me from running further.

Louisa stared out at me.

Her smile had changed.

She was *warning* me. Warning me to stay away from Jonathan.

No!

"Don't get weird, Annie," I scolded myself aloud.

I forced my eyes away from the photograph and hurried around the corner.

Laughter. Up ahead.

I saw Dawn leaning against her locker, books and notebooks at her feet. And I saw Caleb standing close to her.

They were laughing giddily about something.

They stopped when they saw me approaching.

"Got to go," Caleb said, reaching down and picking up some of the books and handing them to Dawn. "How's it going?" he called to me.

"Peachy," I replied sarcastically. "Just peachy."

But Caleb had taken off, waving to Dawn without waiting for my answer.

"Hi, Annie. What's your problem?" Dawn asked, stooping to pick up the rest of her stuff.

"Somebody erased all my work," I blurted out breathlessly.

Dawn straightened up, leaving her books on the floor. "Huh?"

I repeated what I'd said. Her mouth dropped open. She shook her head.

I told her about the warning at the end of the file, telling me to stay away from Jonathan.

Her expression turned thoughtful. She tugged at her hair. "Who would do such a mean thing?" she asked.

I shrugged. "I don't even *know* anyone," I wailed. "This is only my second day in this dumb school!"

"You want to go somewhere and talk about it?" Dawn offered.

"I don't know," I replied miserably. "I think I'll just go home. I'm having a bad day, and — "

I stopped when I saw Jonathan turn the corner. He had his head down and was loping along quickly. A smile spread across his face when he spotted me.

"Hey — hi!" he shouted. He came hurrying up to us, his backpack over one shoulder, a tennis racquet in a blue case in one hand. "What are you guys doing here so late?"

"Caleb had detention, and I had to get some notes from him," Dawn explained.

"Wow. You're in major trouble if you need notes from Caleb!" Jonathan teased her.

"They were *my* notes. I had to get them back from him," Dawn said. She stooped and began picking up her stuff from the floor.

Jonathan turned his attention to me. "What are *you* doing?"

I felt a sudden tremor of fear.

The warning on my computer screen flashed in my mind. And I suddenly saw Louisa's face.

Did you kill her, Jonathan?

The question popped into my mind.

I stared at Jonathan. Was I really afraid of him?

No.

The feeling of fear quickly faded.

He smiled at me warmly, raking his free hand back shyly through his thick hair. His green eyes seemed to smile, too.

Jonathan is no killer, I decided.

"I was up in the computer lab," I told him. "But something happened to my disk. All my work was erased."

"I'm not surprised," Jonathan replied.

"Huh?" I stared at him, startled by his matter-of-fact words. Dawn glanced up at him, too.

"Those old Apples are terrible," Jonathan explained, bouncing the tennis racquet against his shoulder. "They're practically falling apart. My cousin goes to Franklin Heights, and he says they have dozens of brand-new Macs in their computer lab."

"Well, I don't know if it was the computer's fault or not, but all my work is lost," I said unhappily, deciding not to tell him about the warning someone had typed at the end of the file.

Dawn shoved the books and stuff inside her locker, slammed the door, and locked it. "I've got to run." She turned to Jonathan. "What are you doing hanging around so late? You have detention, too?"

He raised his tennis racquet. "Tennis team practice," he told her. "We're going to be all-state this year."

"In your dreams," Dawn muttered sarcastically.

Jonathan's grin grew wider. "No. Really."

"I've got to go," Dawn said, turning to me. "If I'm late for work, they yell at me a lot."

"See you," I said, thinking about my lost notes.

"You want to do something Saturday afternoon?" she called back to me, halfway down the hall. "I have a class in the morning. But later we could drive to the mall or something?"

"I can't," I called back. "Jonathan and I are going to test out my new bike. Want to come along?"

"No thanks. I'm in a shopping mood. See you around." And she disappeared out the side door.

Jonathan and I were alone now, alone in the long, empty hallway. He spun the racquet handle in his hand.

I struggled to think of something to say.

I wondered if I should tell him that I knew about Louisa.

Somehow this didn't seem like the time or the place.

Maybe I'll tell him on Saturday, I thought. Or maybe not.

I mean, what's the point of saying anything about it?

And what could I possibly say?

"Want to walk me home?" I asked, my nervous stammer suddenly returning. "Or would you like me to walk *you* home?"

He smiled, but shook his head. "Can't. I've got to get back to practice. I just came in to make a phone call."

"Okay," I said, shifting my backpack on my shoulders. "See you later. I'm really psyched about Saturday."

"Me, too," he said, twirling the tennis racquet.

We walked together to the side door, our footsteps echoing in the empty corridor. He started to push open the door, then stopped.

He hesitated. Then, to my surprise, he leaned down and kissed me, pushing his lips against mine, softly at first, then harder.

I was so stunned, I swallowed noisily.

Looking over his shoulder as we kissed, I suddenly saw something.

A flash of color.

Someone watching us from the corner where the hallway turned.

I backed away from Jonathan to see better.

Whoever it was pulled back out of sight.

But not before I saw a flash of red hair.

Ruby!

"Come here, Goggles. Come sit on my lap."

I'd been calling to the stubborn cat for ten minutes, but he refused to budge. He just sat in the doorway to the den, staring up at me in the armchair as if I were crazy.

"Okay, stay there," I said crossly, giving up. "Be as unfriendly as you like, you fat furry mop."

As soon as I said that, the contrary animal hurried across the room and leapt into my lap.

I laughed. "I should've used reverse psychology on you before," I told him, stroking the soft, white fur on his back. Goggles put up with me for about a minute, then scampered away.

It was Friday night and I was alone in the house and feeling restless. My parents were at a party at the community college. And my brother Kenny had a sleepover at one of his new friend's.

I tapped my fingers against the arm of the leather chair, trying to decide what to do. There was nothing on TV. The cable hadn't been hooked up yet, so we only had three channels.

I knew I should do more research for my social studies term paper. But I just wasn't in the mood. I mean, who does homework on a Friday night?

"Goggles, where'd you go?" I called.

Then I scolded myself for pestering the cat. Goggles wasn't very good company.

I stood up, thinking maybe I'd do something with my hair. Wash it, then try to style it like that model I saw in a picture in *Seventeen*.

As I started for the doorway, the photo of Louisa flashed into my mind. I saw her hair. It was as blonde as mine, but prettier and wavier. It fell so casually, so naturally. It looked as if she didn't have to fuss with it at all.

She *doesn't* have to fuss with it anymore, I thought grimly.

She's dead.

I tried not to, but for the hundredth time I pictured poor Louisa plunging over the falls with her bike, screaming all the way down. Until she hit the sharp rocks with a sickening *splat*.

No!

Why did I keep imagining that horrifying scene again and again?

Why couldn't I stop thinking about her, about her hideous death?

Think about something pleasant, I told myself.

Force Louisa out of your thoughts. Think about something good that's happening in your life.

And then I thought of Jonathan.

I wondered what he was doing tonight. I

wondered if he was sitting around the house, as bored as I was.

Go ahead. Call him, I urged myself.

I dropped back onto the big armchair and picked up the phone from the end table beside me.

I hesitated.

I suddenly felt nervous.

Go ahead, Annie, I thought. Call him.

What's the big deal?

Holding the receiver, I realized I didn't have Jonathan's phone number. I punched in 411 and asked Information. Then, repeating the number over and over so I wouldn't forget it, I quickly punched it in before I lost my nerve.

It rang once. Twice.

I realized I was squeezing the receiver so tightly, my hand hurt. So I loosened my grip.

Three rings.

He isn't home, I thought, disappointed. No one's home.

Someone picked up in the middle of the fourth ring. "Hello?"

"Uh . . . Mrs. M-Morgan?" I stammered.

"Is that you, Ruby?" Mrs. Morgan asked, sounding surprised. "Hasn't Jonathan picked you up yet? He left for your house a long time ago."

I froze.

My blood seemed to stop flowing. My body turned to granite.

I was a statue. A cold statue.

"Ruby?" Jonathan's mother asked.

"Sorry. I have the wrong n-number," I managed to say. And I slammed down the receiver.

Jonathan is out with Ruby tonight?

I scolded myself for feeling so hurt.

He had a perfect right to go out with Ruby, after all. It wasn't like Jonathan and I . . .

We weren't . . .

He and I never said . . .

I took a deep breath and held it.

I tried to chill out, to stop the angry, upset thoughts from careening through my mind.

I looked down and saw Goggles staring at me from the doorway with those big blue cat eyes.

"Jonathan's out with Ruby tonight," I told the cat.

I jumped a mile as the phone rang. Goggles scampered away.

I picked it up before the second ring.

A harsh, raspy voice began talking before I even said hello.

"Computers don't lie," someone whispered loudly. *"Stay away from Jonathan Morgan. One dead girlfriend is enough."*

Chapter 10

I couldn't get to sleep after that. The raspy, whispering voice kept repeating its crude warning in my mind.

I hadn't been frightened at first.

Sitting in the den, staring at the phone beside me, I'd been more angry than frightened.

Did someone really think they could scare me away from Jonathan by whispering stupid threats over the phone?

The more I thought about it, though, the more frightened I became.

The phone caller knew about the computer. He or she obviously was the one who erased my term paper disk.

And did the caller also slash Kenny's bike tires that afternoon when I met Jonathan?

Whoever it was knew how to reach me, knew where I lived.

I shuddered.

I suddenly remembered a movie I'd seen on TV where a baby-sitter is alone in a house, and she starts getting frightening phone calls — and the caller is upstairs, *right in the house with her!*

I got up and scurried around the house, making sure the doors were locked.

As if that would do any good if someone really wanted to get me.

"It's just a practical joke," I told myself aloud. My trembling voice didn't sound very reassuring.

And again I thought of Louisa.

She was *really* dead. No practical joke.

Later, I went to bed and couldn't get to sleep.

The shadows on my ceiling looked like dark, pointed rocks.

I stared up at them wide-eyed, feeling the fear choke my throat, hearing the whispered threat over the phone, the raspy voice like water rushing over the falls.

Somehow I eventually fell asleep.

The next morning, I called Dawn right after breakfast. I *had* to talk to someone.

"I'm rushing out," she said, surprised to hear from me so early. "I have this stupid electrical engineering class on Saturday mornings."

"You have *what*?" I demanded, certain that I hadn't heard her correctly.

"You heard me," she replied, groaning. "It's a beginner's course in electrical wiring and stuff. At the Y. It's two hours every Saturday morning. You see, Ruby thinks that girls should know how to do junk like that. You know. Have skills. And she talked me into taking the class with her."

"How did she ever do that?" I asked.

"Well, the instructor's this really cute guy. . . ." Dawn started. She sighed. "I don't know. We've only done it a couple of weeks. It's kind of interesting. Circuits and stuff."

"Weird," I said.

"What's up?" she asked.

"I got this call last night," I said. I told her about the frightening call. The threat.

"That's really gross!" Dawn exclaimed. "Did you tell your parents?"

"Well . . . no," I replied.

"Maybe you should tell them," Dawn urged. "Whoever this nut is, he might be serious. I think your parents should know."

"What makes you think it's a *he*?" I asked.

Dawn was silent for a moment. I could practically hear her brain working over the phone line. "Why? Who do you think it is?" she asked finally.

"Ruby, maybe," I said.

I hadn't really thought about it before that second. I hadn't really suspected Ruby.

But, suddenly, the whispered, raspy voice sounded a lot like Ruby's to me.

"Ruby?" Dawn sounded stunned. "Hey, Annie, I don't think so."

"But, Dawn — "

"Ruby's okay," Dawn interrupted. "You shouldn't trust first impressions. She's really okay."

"Well, you know her better than I do," I said reluctantly. "But something about the whispered voice . . ."

"Come on. Why would Ruby try to scare you away from Jonathan?" Dawn demanded.

"Well, for one thing, they went out together last night," I said.

"Huh?"

Dawn sounded really shocked.

"Are you sure?" she asked breathlessly.

"Yeah, I'm sure." I told Dawn about my phone call to Jonathan's house, and how Mrs. Morgan mistook me for Ruby.

"Wow," Dawn kept repeating. "Wow."

"How come you're so surprised?" I demanded.

It took her a while to answer. "It's sort of a long story," she said. "I'm just surprised, that's all. I'll have to ask Ruby all about their date at our class. I'll tell you about it later. I'm late."

"But, Dawn — "

"Are you still going bike riding with Jonathan this afternoon?" she asked.

"Yeah. I guess."

"Well, be careful, okay?" And then Dawn hung up.

Be careful?

I stared at the humming phone receiver. What did she mean?

Be careful of *what*? Of Jonathan?

Jonathan arrived a little before two. I watched from the living room window as he sped up our driveway on his bike and leapt off while it was still going, letting the bike topple to the grass.

He didn't see me. I watched him from the window as he pulled down his pale blue sweatshirt and pushed back his hair with both hands.

It was kind of fun spying on him.

He's so great-looking, I thought. He should be in Hollywood starring on TV shows.

I suddenly remembered something my mom had said a long time ago about not hanging around with boys who were better-looking than I was.

It's funny the things that pop into your mind for no reason at all.

The front doorbell rang. I hurried across the room and pulled open the door.

Jonathan seemed really glad to see me. We talked for a few minutes, just making small talk. I pulled a long green blade of grass from his hair. "How'd you get this?" I asked, twirling it in my fingers.

"Mowing the lawn this morning," he groaned. "My dad always has to be the first on his block. Only *I'm* the one who has to do the mowing." He scratched his head, frowning. "And, then, Dad says since we mowed so early in the season, we have to rake. Only *I'm* the one who does the raking. I'm totally wrecked!"

"So you don't want to go riding?" I asked, unable to conceal my disappointment.

He laughed. "No. I *need* to go riding. Just as long as we don't ride on *grass*!"

My mom came by, carrying one of the still-unpacked cartons from the back. I introduced Jonathan to her. She set down the carton and shook his hand. I could tell by the look on her face that she was impressed with how good-looking he was.

A short while later, I pulled my new bike out of the garage and walked it over to Jonathan on the driveway.

It was a warm, sunny day with a few puffy

clouds in the sky. The air was heavy and wet, almost like summer.

"Excellent bike!" Jonathan exclaimed, rubbing his hand along the shiny blue frame. "Really excellent!"

"You can't tell it's used, can you?" I asked. "It has one tiny scratch on the side here. That's all."

He admired the bike for a while longer. "It's a ten-speed?"

"No. Twenty-one."

"Excellent." He raised his eyes to mine. "Let's get going."

"Great," I said enthusiastically. I lifted my leg over the frame and straddled the bike, preparing to glide down the driveway. "Where shall we go?"

He narrowed his eyes in concentration. "Well . . ."

The sun disappeared behind one of the puffy clouds. A shadow rolled over us. The air immediately grew cooler.

I felt a sudden chill as Jonathan stared into my eyes and said, "Let's ride up to the falls."

Chapter 11

Why did I feel that cold shiver of fear when Jonathan suggested we ride up to the falls?

I was angry at myself for feeling it.

I had no reason to be afraid of Jonathan. He seemed to really like me.

A horrible thing had happened up at the falls. But that was no reason to be frightened of Jonathan.

I reasoned that Jonathan was trying to get over Louisa, trying to get over her death.

By returning to the falls with me, he was forcing himself to get on with his life. He was putting Louisa behind him, putting all of the horror behind him.

That was my reasoning. I wished I had the courage to ask Jonathan if I was right. But I didn't feel I knew him well enough yet to bring it up.

He had never mentioned Louisa to me.

I didn't think it was right for me to be the first to bring her up.

We rode in the middle of the street. There was little traffic. Lawns were being mowed. And raked. Flowers were being planted. Gardens were being tended. Weeds were being pulled.

A group of little kids were gleefully climbing through the open walls of a new house being built. "This is *my* room!" a little boy cried. "No — that's the kitchen!" another boy corrected him.

"How you doing?" Jonathan called back to me. He had gotten about three car-lengths ahead.

"Fine. I like this bike," I shouted.

"That's Caleb's house, remember?" Jonathan said, pointing to a square, white clapboard house with a ragged low hedge running along the front.

And just as Jonathan pointed, Caleb appeared on the gravel driveway. "Hey!" he called, spotting us immediately. "Where you going?"

Jonathan wheeled around and pedaled onto the drive, his tires sliding over the gravel as he hit the brakes. His front tire came to a stop less than an inch from Caleb who, grinning, raised both hands over his head in surrender.

I pulled up beside Jonathan and lowered both feet to the gravel.

"Hot day, huh?" Caleb said, grinning at me, pushing his scraggly hair back off his forehead. The gold earring in his ear sparkled in the sunlight.

"Why don't we talk about the weather for a while," Jonathan said sarcastically. He gazed up at Caleb's house. Someone was watching us from the front window. Caleb's mom, I guess. "You get your bike fixed?" Jonathan asked.

"Pretty much," Caleb replied, grinning.

"Want to come with us?" Jonathan offered.

Caleb nodded. "I haven't had any better offers." He wiped his hands off on the legs of his jeans. "I'll get my bike. The tires are low, but that's okay."

He started toward the back of the house, kicking up the gravel as he walked. After a few steps, he turned back. "Where we riding?"

"Up to the falls," I answered.

"Huh?" Caleb's mouth dropped open. "What did you say?" His eyes were on Jonathan.

"Up to the falls," I repeated softly, surprised by Caleb's reaction.

Caleb continued to stare at Jonathan. "You sure?"

"Yeah. We're sure," Jonathan snapped.

"You coming before suppertime or not? My bike is rusting, waiting for you."

"Hey, you're in a good mood," Caleb muttered. "Sure you want me to come along?"

"Get your bike," Jonathan instructed him.

Caleb disappeared around the back of the house. "Someone should mow Caleb's lawn," I said, gazing at the tall, overgrown grass and flourishing weeds.

"His parents won't trust him with a lawn-mower," Jonathan replied, grinning. "They know he'd probably cut his foot off."

After a short while, Caleb came sailing down on a rickety old BMX bike, the seat raised up as high as it would go, both tires nearly flat. "To the falls!" he cried, rolling past us, out of the driveway and into the street without slowing to look for cars.

"He's really messed up," Jonathan muttered to me, shaking his head.

Caleb was twirling his bike in tight circles, waiting for us, singing at the top of his lungs.

"He's your best friend," I said dryly.

"Why?" Jonathan asked, making a bewildered face.

Laughing, we followed Caleb into the street. We pedaled single file to town, which was crowded and busy, with cars actually double-parked on Main Street. Most people were going into the garden store and the hardware store. Spring fix-up time.

Past town, the road started to climb through the woods. Jonathan and I rode side by side behind Caleb, who zigzagged wildly from one side of the road to the other, riding no-hands most of the time.

After a bit, the road leveled out, and I could see a large red truck coming toward us in the near distance.

"Hey, get over!" Jonathan called to Caleb. Caleb was riding no-hands in the left lane, the lane the truck was in.

Staying in the wrong lane, Caleb turned back to us, a devilish grin on his face, his dark eyes glowing. "Watch what I do to this guy," he called.

"No way! Get over!" Jonathan screamed.

The red truck, an enormous van, seemed to grow larger as it approached.

"Watch!" Caleb cried.

"Get over!" Jonathan screamed.

Caleb stayed on the wrong side, pedaling steadily, calmly, as if he had every right to be there, as if there wasn't a huge truck barreling right at him.

"This is stupid!" Jonathan screamed. His eyes were bugging out with fright.

The trunk honked its horn, a long, earth shaking diesel honk.

"Get over, idiot!" I could barely hear Jonathan's shout over the roar of the truck horn.

A wild grin on his face, Caleb just kept pedaling.

The truck wasn't slowing down. It rumbled closer. Closer.

"Caleb — please!"

I closed my eyes as the blaring horn became an angry, deafening scream.

Chapter 12

The ground seemed to shake.

I felt a powerful rush of hot air, which nearly blew me over.

When I opened my eyes, I saw Caleb seated on his bike, both feet on the dirt on the other side of the road. He grinned at Jonathan and me and raised his fists triumphantly, cheering loudly for himself.

Jonathan tossed down his bike and angrily strode across the road to Caleb. I could hear the truck rumbling away from us. It still felt to me as if the ground were shaking.

My heart was thudding in my chest. I felt dizzy. Straddling my bike, I stared across the road at Caleb as if he were a mirage.

"You could've been killed, man!" Jonathan screamed angrily at him.

"No way," Caleb insisted, his arms crossed

over his chest, his face bearing its usual goofy grin. "I've got timing."

"Timing? You're crazy!" Jonathan insisted.

"It's all timing," Caleb bragged, ignoring Jonathan's anger. Caleb turned his eyes to me. "Did you see the look on that truck driver's face?"

"No, I didn't see anything," I admitted. "I closed my eyes." My legs were all trembly. My mouth was dry.

"I thought his face was going to explode!" Caleb laughed.

"That was real dumb," Jonathan said, scowling.

"I didn't get hit, did I?" Caleb demanded. "If I got hit, *that* would be dumb. If I'm lying here flat as a pancake, then *that's* dumb. But I've got the timing down. You know that, Jonathan."

Jonathan glared angrily at Caleb. He leaned close to his friend and lowered his voice. But I heard what he said anyway. He told Caleb, "You're just showing off for Annie."

"Huh? Who — me?" Caleb glanced over Jonathan's shoulder at me. "No way, Jonathan."

Jonathan tossed up his hands, as if conceding defeat. "Are we going to ride or not?"

"Yeah. Sure. Let's go," Caleb replied, sounding hurt.

Jonathan walked quickly across the road, picked up his bike, and climbed onto it without looking at me. I could see that his mood had changed. Caleb's game of chicken with the truck had really upset him.

"He could have bought it that time," Jonathan muttered, more to himself than to me.

We started to pedal, slowly picking up speed as the road curved through the woods, climbing toward the falls.

"Why does Caleb like to play such dangerous games?" I asked.

"Because I'm a dangerous guy!" Caleb exclaimed, overhearing me. He laughed gleefully. "I'm so *dangerous*!"

Jonathan just scowled.

A few minutes later, we turned off the road onto the bike path that led up to the top of the falls.

The falls were more beautiful than I'd remembered, the water sparkling like silver under the sun as it washed straight down from the cliff edge.

"It smells so fresh and clean up here," I said, closing my eyes and taking a deep breath.

We left our bikes on the bike path. I turned away from the falls to look at the woods. The leaves were all opening. The woods were so much brighter and greener than the week before.

I hoped that the beautiful scenery would help return Jonathan's good spirits. But when I turned back to the falls, I was startled to see that he had stepped right to the cliff edge and was peering down, a grim expression on his face.

That's just where he'd stood when I first met him, I realized, feeling a sudden wave of dread sweep over my body.

That's just where he stood. On the very edge. Staring down so sadly.

I had thought then that Jonathan was going to jump.

I could feel my face grow hot, remembering that.

I suddenly became aware that Caleb had moved beside me. He was staring at Jonathan, too.

"I knew we shouldn't have come up here," Caleb said to me in a low voice, keeping his eyes on Jonathan. "I knew he wasn't ready to come up here yet."

"He was in a really good mood before," I

said, feeling the cold spray off the falls on my face.

"Now he's not," Caleb said sharply, shaking his head. "We shouldn't be here."

He moved away from me and headed toward Jonathan, stopping a few feet from the edge. "Hey, Jonathan — ?"

Jonathan didn't turn around. He stood motionless, staring straight down into the streaming rush of white water.

"Jonathan, let's go," Caleb insisted, reaching out a hand as if intending to pull Jonathan away.

No reaction.

"Jonathan, let's go — okay?"

I took a few steps closer, suddenly very worried about Jonathan.

What was he thinking about?

What was he looking for?

Why wouldn't he answer Caleb?

Why wouldn't he step back from the cliff edge?

I stepped up beside Caleb, who looked really worried. I think it was the first time I had seen Caleb with a serious expression on his face.

"Jonathan — ?" he called. "Earth calling Jonathan."

"Just a second," Jonathan said, not turning around.

"Come on, man," Caleb urged.

"Just a second," Jonathan repeated. "That's all it takes. A second. A split second. And then you're dead. Gone forever."

Caleb glanced at me, his features tight with worry. Then he grabbed Jonathan by the shoulder and pulled him back.

"Hey, what's the problem? Let go!" Jonathan protested.

"You're scaring us, man," Caleb told him, not letting go. He was pulling Jonathan back from the cliff edge with both hands.

The spray drenched my face and hair. I suddenly felt cold, despite the bright sun overhead.

"I'm okay," Jonathan insisted.

"I don't like to hear you talking like that," Caleb said.

"Let's keep riding," I suggested, trying to sound cheerful.

"Yeah. Good idea," Caleb said.

I turned toward the bike path and screamed. "Hey — !"

Someone was back there, messing with my bike.

"Hey — get away!" I screamed.

Brushing the spray from my eyes, I began running to my bike.

The intruder had picked my bike up off the ground and was doing something to the handlebars.

I had only gone a few steps when I recognized who it was.

Ruby!

Chapter 13

"Hey — get away!"

My sneakers pounded the dirt, kicking up dust as I ran toward Ruby. I could hear Jonathan and Caleb running behind me.

"Huh?" Ruby stood holding my bike by the handlebars, staring at me openmouthed, her red hair disheveled, gleaming in the bright sunlight.

I pulled up in front of her, gasping for breath. "What are you doing to my bike?" I demanded angrily.

"I'm just *looking* at it," she snapped back. "It's a lot like my cousin's bike."

I glared at her angrily, trying to catch my breath.

"I wasn't going to steal it or anything," she said, turning her snub nose up.

"What's the problem?" Caleb asked, running up beside me.

"Annie thought I was going to run away with her bike," Ruby told him, frowning. "I just wanted to look at it. Here." She pushed the bike toward me.

I grabbed the frame and the seat to keep it from toppling over. "Ruby, I'm sorry — " I started.

"I'm not a thief, you know," Ruby said nastily.

"Hey, Annie didn't mean it," Caleb said, trying to be helpful.

"Remember? Someone slashed my tires last week," I told Ruby. "That's why I thought — "

"Well, it wasn't me!" Ruby interrupted.

I felt really embarrassed. I'd come running after Ruby like a crazy person, screaming at her, accusing her. And she was just looking at the bike.

"I'm really sorry," I said sincerely. "Really. I didn't mean — "

"Okay, okay," Ruby said impatiently. Her bike was lying on its side a few feet down the bike path. She picked it up and walked it back toward the tall granite rocks.

I wheeled mine after her, and Caleb followed.

"Where is Dawn?" Ruby asked, shielding her eyes from the sun with one hand as her eyes followed the curve of the sloping bike path.

"Is Dawn with you?" Caleb asked, following Ruby's gaze.

"Here she comes," Ruby announced.

I saw Dawn, standing up as she pedaled, moving slowly up the hill. A few seconds later, she hopped off her bike and walked it up to us. She was red-faced and out of breath. Her dark hair was wet, a large strand matted against her perspiring forehead.

"Wow. I'm a little out of shape," she exclaimed breathlessly. "I've *got* to lose some weight."

"You look okay," Caleb said gallantly. He laughed. "You just need a better bike. Yours is too heavy. You should get one like Annie's."

"But don't touch Annie's, whatever you do," Ruby warned sarcastically, flashing me a dirty look. "If you touch her bike, she freaks."

"Huh?" Dawn gazed at me, puzzled.

I leaned back against the rocks. "I made a mistake," I muttered. "I didn't mean — "

"Did you get that bike new or used?" Ruby asked.

"Used," I told her.

"It looks brand-new," she said.

"It was such a pretty day," Dawn said, pushing the hair off her forehead. "I told Ruby we should ride up. I was hoping you'd still be here."

"It's cooler up here," Ruby said.

"We should keep riding," Caleb suggested. "Keep going to Cedar, maybe."

"I want to cool off a bit, first," Dawn said, leaning her bike against the rocks.

"You know, we should start a bike club," Caleb said with great enthusiasm.

"Huh?" Dawn narrowed her eyes at him.

"Yeah. A bike club," he repeated, undiscouraged. "We're just about the only ones in Shocklin Falls who like to ride around everywhere on our bikes, right?"

"Give me a break, Caleb," Dawn said, rolling her eyes. "You ride that beat-up bike of yours because you can't afford a car, and your parents won't trust you with theirs."

"Smart parents," Ruby muttered, grinning.

"Hey, no way," Caleb protested. "I'm really into bikes, you know."

Dawn made a sarcastic face.

"I'm just saying we could get together every weekend or something and maybe ride all over the state. You know, plan different routes. Bring food and stuff."

"I like the food part," I said, starting to feel hungry. I hadn't had much of a lunch.

"Forget it," Dawn told Caleb. "I *hate* riding with you. You're too crazy. Always showing off. Trying to get yourself killed."

"Who? *Me?*" Caleb protested, grinning.

He had somehow conveniently forgotten about his little game of chicken with the truck a short while before.

"Hey, where's Jonathan?" Ruby asked suddenly. "Isn't he up here with you?"

Jonathan.

I was so worked up about Ruby and my bike, I had forgotten all about Jonathan!

"He was with you," I told Caleb.

"No," Caleb replied. "I don't think so."

We all turned toward the falls.

No one there.

The water roared down, a fine white spray rising from the cliff edge.

"Jonathan!" I called. "Jonathan, where are you?"

No reply.

I turned toward the woods. No sign of him.

When I turned back, Caleb was running to the cliff edge, a frightened expression on his face.

Dawn and Ruby were staring at me. "Where *is* he?" Ruby demanded, as if I were hiding him.

A wave of dread swept over me. Heavy fear, weighing me down, making it hard to breathe.

I raised my eyes to Caleb, standing at the cliff edge over the falls.

The exact spot where Jonathan had been standing.

Caleb peered straight down, his features twisted in fear. "Did he jump?" he cried. "Did Jonathan jump?"

Behind me, Ruby uttered a high-pitched scream of horror.

Chapter 14

"No! No!" I heard a frightened voice shriek.

It took me a while to realize it was *me*!

Caleb took a step back from the falls. "I don't see anything down there," he called, cupping his hands over his mouth to be heard over the roaring waterfall.

"Look!" Ruby cried.

We turned to the bike path.

There was Jonathan. On his bike. Dust flew up on both sides of his bike as he pedaled furiously away.

The four of us stood frozen in silence, staring after him, watching him disappear into the trees.

He never looked back.

When he vanished from view, I let out a long sigh of relief and dropped to my knees onto the ground.

At least Jonathan hadn't jumped.

I raised my eyes to Ruby and Dawn. Dawn had tears in her eyes. Her shoulders were trembling. "I — I was so scared!" she stammered.

Ruby put a hand on Dawn's shoulder to calm her.

"I mean, first Louisa. Then . . ." Dawn's voice trailed off.

Caleb made his way back to us, his hands shoved into his jeans pockets, his head lowered.

"Why'd he do that?" I asked him, my heart still pounding. "Why'd Jonathan run away like that?"

Caleb shrugged grimly. "Beats me."

"I really thought he jumped," Ruby said in a quivering voice.

"Do you think he's *mad* at us for some reason?" Dawn wondered. She leaned back against the rocks and pushed her damp hair off her face. She looked very pale, very upset.

"I *knew* we shouldn't have come up here," Caleb said heatedly. "It was too soon for Jonathan."

"But he had already come up here," I told Caleb. "Last week. I — "

"Was it *your* idea?" Caleb demanded loudly, staring angrily at me.

I gasped.

In that instant, I realized that Caleb didn't like me.

His outburst cut through me. I felt a stab of pain in my chest.

He doesn't like me, I thought, staring up at him, studying his angry expression.

"No. It wasn't my idea," I replied coldly, turning away from him.

"Well, it was a bad idea," Caleb insisted. "Don't you have any idea what Jonathan's been through?"

"Give her a break, Caleb," Dawn said, coming to my defense. "Annie knows the whole story."

"Let's get out of here," Ruby suggested, pushing away from the rocks and reaching for her bike. "Let's ride somewhere else, okay? This place gives me the creeps. I keep picturing Louisa standing there."

"Yeah. Let's keep riding," Dawn quickly agreed.

"I — I think I'd better get home," I told them. "I'm so behind on my term paper. I threw away the notes I'd typed onto the disk. And then it was all erased. I'm practically starting all over again."

"You sure?" Dawn asked, pulling up her bike. "It's too nice out to be stuck inside doing schoolwork."

"I know," I sighed. "But I'd better do it."

"Don't be upset about Jonathan," Dawn said as I retrieved my bike. "He's moody." She chuckled. "I guess you've noticed."

I said good-bye to them and headed down the hill, pedaling hard.

I *am* upset about Jonathan, I thought unhappily.

I'm *very* upset.

I thought this was a date. Why did he ride away and leave me there without saying a word?

Why did he do it?

That night, I had a frightening nightmare.

The dream was in black and white. Somehow the darkness of it, the somber gray shadows, made it all the more horrifying.

In the dream, I was standing at the falls.

The water rushed down silently.

The whole dream was silent. Not a sound. Not a voice.

I stared at the rushing water, watched it plunge to the dark rocks below without making a splash.

It was cold up there. A wet chill fell over me, over everything. The sky was a cold charcoal-gray, a dead gray.

Someone stood at the edge of the cliff. Someone dressed in black.

I stared at her and listened to the silence.

Mist rose up from the plunging waters, gray and cold.

Even with her back turned to me, I realized it was Louisa.

I called to her, but no sound came out of my throat.

She turned around slowly.

I stared at her face.

I uttered a silent scream.

Her skin was gone. Her beautiful, wavy hair rested on top of a grinning skeleton.

Empty eye sockets stared at me blindly.

Her jawbone lowered, revealing a mouth full of perfect white teeth.

She turned quickly away from me.

Once again, she resumed her stance at the edge of the falls.

The water continued to sweep down in total silence.

The sky darkened. Shadows rolled over the hard, gray ground.

I crept up silently behind Louisa.

Closer. Closer still.

I knew what I was going to do.

I raised my hands.

I was going to shove her over the edge.

Hands ready, I took another step. Another.

Suddenly, my voice returned. I spoke.

"I'm Jonathan's new girlfriend," I said as I prepared to push Louisa. "I'm Jonathan's girlfriend now."

I said the words in a flat monotone, without any emotion at all.

The water flowed down, down, down. Silently.

I reached forward. I started to push her.

But as my hands lowered to her back, we suddenly changed places.

To my horror, I realized that I was now dressed in black.

I was now standing at the very edge of the silent falls.

"I'm Jonathan's new girlfriend," I said. "I'm Jonathan's dead girlfriend."

Was Louisa behind me now?

Was Jonathan?

I couldn't turn around. I could only look down.

I knew that I was about to go over the edge, into the silently plunging waters.

I knew that I was about to die.

Silently. So silently.

Into the gray churning shadows below.

The ringing of the phone by my bed woke me up.

I sat up, startled, wide awake.

The dream faded slowly. The gray shadows lingered.

I blinked. Once. Twice.

The phone continued to ring.

I reached for it, then hesitated.

The cold fear I felt — was it from the dream? Or from the ringing of the phone?

Should I answer it?

Reluctantly, I lifted the receiver to my ear.

"It's me," said a dry, whispered voice.

Chapter 15

My breath caught in my throat.

I shut my eyes.

"Annie?" the voice whispered. "Is that you?"

I swallowed hard.

"It's me. Jonathan," the voice whispered.

"Huh?" I cried. "Jonathan?"

"Who'd you *think* it was?" he asked, still whispering.

"What time is it?" I asked, squinting through the darkness at my clock radio. "Jonathan, it's nearly two."

"Oh. Sorry."

"Why are you whispering like that?" I demanded, my heart slowing to a normal pace.

"I don't want my parents to hear," he replied. "They'll take away my phone if they hear me calling so late."

"You scared me," I admitted. "I thought — I thought you were someone else."

"I just called to apologize," Jonathan said. "You know. For this afternoon."

"Okay. Go ahead," I said. "Apologize."

"I apologize," he said earnestly.

I chuckled. "Apology accepted," I told him. "You could've called earlier, you know."

"I wanted to, but I had to go somewhere with my dad. Listen, Annie, I shouldn't have run off like that. But . . . well . . . it's hard to explain."

"That's okay," I said, hearing how hard this was for him.

I was so relieved that he wasn't mad at me, that he didn't blame me for some reason.

"I shouldn't have suggested that we go up there," he continued. "I mean, it was just too soon. You probably don't know about Louisa — "

"Yes. I heard," I interrupted.

He was silent for a long moment. "Yeah. I guess everyone talks about it," he said finally, with some bitterness.

"Dawn told me . . . about Louisa," I said softly.

As I said it, the dream washed over me. Again I saw the silent falls, the shifting gray shadows, the girl dressed in black, standing on the very edge, about to fall.

Was it Louisa — or was it me?

"You want to get together tomorrow?" Jonathan asked, abruptly changing the subject. "We could go to a movie or something."

"I wish I could," I replied.

"I won't run away. Promise!" he quickly added.

"I've got to work on my research," I said. "I'll never get that paper written at this rate."

"Oh. I see." He sounded very disappointed.

"Sorry," I said, and then I yawned loudly.

"Guess I'd better hang up," he whispered.

"I'm glad you called," I said honestly.

We said good-night and hung up.

I lowered my head to the pillow and pulled up the blanket.

When I closed my eyes, images from my frightening dream returned, as if they'd been waiting for me.

No, I thought, opening my eyes wide, trying to drive the pictures away. No, I don't want to think about Louisa now. I don't want to think about this.

"Jonathan didn't push Louisa," I whispered to myself, staring up at the dark ceiling. "Jonathan didn't push her. I *know* he didn't!"

I had just gotten down to work the next afternoon, papers and books spread out all over the dining room table, when the doorbell rang.

Since I was the only one home, I ran to answer it.

"Dawn!" I cried out in surprise.

She smiled at me. She was wearing a blue sweater over white tennis shorts. Her hair was tied loosely behind her head.

"I really have to work," I told her, holding open the screen door. "I don't have time to — "

"I know," she said, stepping past me into the front hallway. "I brought you a bunch of books." She lowered her shoulder so I could see the bulging backpack on her back. "You know. For research."

"Hey, thanks," I cried, genuinely grateful. "That's really nice of you. The library is closed on Sundays, so — "

"I think it's all stuff you can use," she said, groaning as she pulled the backpack off.

I led her into the dining room, and she emptied the contents of the backpack onto the table. "I'll only stay for a minute," she said, pulling out a chair and sitting down. "Have you talked to Jonathan?"

I told her about his late-night apology.

"Weird," she said. And, then, fiddling with her hair, she added, "Poor guy." Her expression changed to anger. "I've just about *had* it with his pal Caleb."

"Huh? What do you mean?" I asked, sifting through the books she had brought, glancing at the titles.

"He's just impossible," Dawn complained, frowning. "He's such a goof. He can never be serious. We went to the movies last night, and he called out funny remarks through the whole picture. The people around us were really angry. They didn't think he was funny at all. I thought they were going to punch his lights out."

I tsk-tsked, only half-concentrating on what Dawn was saying. I really did want to get back to work.

"Caleb's parents actually let him take the car last night," Dawn continued, sighing unhappily. "They haven't let him drive it in weeks. So what did he do? He drove it into a ditch, and we had to be towed. *Aaaaagh!*" She uttered a cry of total frustration, pounding both fists on the table.

"What a drag," I said, trying to sound sympathetic. "Caleb really is a crazy guy."

"I'm going to make a change," Dawn said, locking her eyes on mine. I had the feeling that she had made up her mind just that second. "I'm going to break up with him. I really am. I don't know why I've put up with him for so long."

She climbed to her feet and picked up her empty backpack. She started to the doorway, then stopped. "Don't say anything, Annie. To Caleb, I mean. Or to anyone."

"Okay," I agreed.

"In case I chicken out or change my mind," Dawn said.

I suppose I should have said something nice about Caleb. Maybe that's what Dawn wanted. Maybe she was confiding in me so that I'd defend Caleb and make her change her mind about breaking up with him.

But I remembered Caleb's angry outburst, the way he shouted at me up at the falls. I remembered the intense look of dislike on his face as he glared at me.

And I guess I had decided that I didn't like Caleb, either.

So I didn't defend him.

Dawn left, determined to break up with him. Before the screen door had slammed behind her, I had buried myself in my research books.

I worked for a couple of hours, but my mind kept wandering. The hideous dream wouldn't fade away. It kept invading my thoughts. And I found myself daydreaming about Jonathan, making up conversations with him in my mind.

My thoughts wandered to Louisa. I wondered what she was like, what her voice sounded like, what her laugh was like.

I glanced up at the clock. It was a little past four, and I hadn't covered much ground at all with my research.

I stood up and stretched, feeling restless.

I couldn't sit there anymore. I had to get out, get some exercise. I had to clear my mind.

I pulled a long-sleeved shirt over my T-shirt and hurried outside to get my bike out of the garage. It was a gray, overcast day. Heavy, dark clouds hovered menacingly low. I could hear the rumble of thunder in the distance.

But I didn't care. I had to ride for a while. Maybe a long while.

As I pedaled down the drive and into the street, the cool, damp air felt good against my hot cheeks. The wind brushed my hair back as I stood up and pedaled harder, picking up speed.

Faster. Faster.

I wanted to ride faster than my thoughts. I wanted to ride away from the frightening dream, from Louisa's smiling face — from everything and everyone.

Houses and lawns rolled past in a gray-green blur. A little kid in a yellow rainslicker waved to me from his driveway, and I waved back but didn't slow my pace.

Faster. Faster.

My heart was pounding. I could feel the blood pulsing at my temples.

There were cold drops of rain in the air. The sky grew even darker.

I rode past the high school, then turned onto a walk that led around the school. The walk ended behind the faculty parking lot, dark and empty.

The distant thunder had become a steady rumble, moving closer. I headed my bike along the dirt path that led into the woods behind the school.

I hadn't had a chance to explore these woods. Someone had told me they stretched on forever.

The tall trees with their freshly unfurled leaves blocked out most of the remaining light. I felt a sudden flash of fear as I realized it was nearly as dark as night here.

But I couldn't stop riding. I wasn't ready to turn around. It felt so good to be speeding through the cold air, under the dark trees.

At first, the only sounds were the whisper of the trees, the low rumble of thunder, and the scud of my bike tires along the curving dirt path.

But then I heard another sound.

Behind me.

Close behind me.

I turned and saw someone on the path. Someone dressed in dark clothes.

Running.

Running after me.

My dream suddenly flashed into my mind. All black and white.

Black and white like the figure chasing me.

Panic gripped my legs.

I wanted to speed up, to get away from the dark dream.

He was closing the gap, running at full speed, his shoes slapping the dirt noisily.

"Ohh!"

I cried out as my front tire hit something in the path. A rock, probably.

I didn't have time to see it.

The bike flew out of control.

I saw the trees tilt. Then the ground came up to meet me.

I landed hard on my side with a jolt of pain that ran up and down my entire body.

The bike fell on top of me, the front tire spinning rapidly.

He's got me, I thought.

Chapter 16

My heart thudding in my chest, I tried frantically to push the bike off me.

I heard my pursuer's footsteps stop. He was standing over me.

I glanced up.

"Ryan!" I cried.

Breathing hard, he bent down, grabbed the handlebars, and pulled the bike away.

He leaned it against a tree, then wiped perspiration off his forehead with the sleeve of his black sweatshirt.

"Ryan — what are you *doing* here?" I demanded in a high-pitched, shrill voice I barely recognized.

He took my arm and helped me up. "Are you okay?" he asked, ignoring my question. "Are you hurt?"

"No, I don't think so," I replied shakily. I tried to brush the mud off the leg of my jeans.

It started to rain. First I heard the *tap-tap-tap* of raindrops on the leaves overhead. Then I felt large, cold drops on my hair.

"Why'd you run away?" Ryan asked, staring at me through his glasses, a bewildered expression on his slender face.

"I — I don't know," I admitted, embarrassed. "I thought you were — "

Someone from my dream?

What *did* I think?

Why *did* I panic like that?

"I thought I was alone," I explained. "When I saw someone chasing me . . ."

"Didn't you hear me calling you?" he asked. He pulled a leafy twig off the sleeve of my shirt.

The pattering of raindrops against the leaves grew louder. I could feel the rain on my shoulders now. "We're going to get soaked," I said. I picked up my bike and examined it. It seemed okay. It wasn't bent or anything. "I think I hit a rock."

"Yeah," Ryan agreed. He pointed to the path. A square-shaped stone jutted up right in the center of the dirt. "You were really moving!" Ryan exclaimed, still studying my face intently.

"Yeah," I said, starting to catch my breath. "So what were you doing here?"

I began walking my bike back toward the

school. Ryan followed, walking close beside me.

"Louisa and I used to walk here all the time," he told me, turning his eyes to the trees up ahead. "This was where we used to hang out."

I waited for him to continue, but he didn't. We walked on in silence for a while.

The rain was cold but gentle. The trees shook as if shivering. My hair was soaked, but it felt refreshing. Cleansing, somehow.

"Louisa was such a good friend," Ryan said, breaking the silence. His expression was thoughtful. His narrow shoulders were hunched under his sweatshirt as he trudged along beside me, hands shoved in his jeans pockets. He avoided my eyes.

I think he expected me to reply, but I didn't know what to say.

"We used to talk about everything," he went on. "She told me things she'd *never* tell Jonathan." A strange smile formed on Ryan's face. He kept his eyes straight ahead.

I wondered if what he'd said was true.

Why was he telling me this now?

I barely knew him. I'd only talked with him once. Why was he confiding in me?

He seems terribly lonely, I realized.

"She was my best friend," he said softly. He stopped suddenly. He grabbed my shoulder, forcing me to stop. I nearly dropped my bike.

Ryan turned his eyes to mine in an intense stare. "I want *you* to be my friend, too," he said with emotion.

"W-well . . ." I stammered. He was squeezing my arm so hard, it hurt. "Ryan, I — "

"I want you to be my good friend, too."

Still squeezing my shoulder, he pressed his face against mine and tried to kiss me.

I was so startled!

My breath caught in my throat.

His lips felt hot and dry against mine. He pressed them against me too hard, too desperately.

He was really hurting me.

With a bit of a struggle, I shoved him away. "Ryan — stop!"

He looked surprised for a moment, then hurt.

I felt terribly confused. And frightened.

He was so violent. So needy.

I jumped on my bike and started to pedal, standing up. "Bye," I shouted, without turning back.

The rain flew into my face, coming down heavier now. Thunder roared nearby, seeming to shake the dark trees.

"You'll be sorry if you hang around with Jonathan!" I heard Ryan shout. "You'll be sorry!"

I turned back to make sure he wasn't chasing after me.

Thunder roared.

"Poor Louisa!" Ryan shouted as it echoed through the trees. "She was sorry. I tried to warn her!"

He shouted something else, but it was drowned out by thunder.

I was too far away to hear him now. The back of the school came into view with a flash of bright white lightning.

I pedaled faster, soaked to the skin.

"Ryan's crazy," I said into the wind, his voice still lingering in my ears. "Ryan's really crazy."

After school on Monday, I was on my way to the computer lab. It was going to be my hangout for the rest of the week. I was determined to get all my research notes typed in so that I could organize them and then start writing my paper.

If only I had my own computer at home, I thought.

My birthday was only a week away. But with all the expenses of moving into a new house, I knew my parents wouldn't buy me a computer.

As I hurried down the hallway toward the lab, kids were pulling out their backpacks, slamming their lockers shut, and heading out of the building.

I saw Ruby speeding off in the other

direction, her red hair disheveled, an intense, thoughtful expression on her face. "Hey, Ruby!" I called to her as she passed.

But she didn't seem to hear me. She kept right on going.

What's *her* problem? I wondered.

For a brief moment, I suspected that she had deliberately ignored me. But I decided that couldn't be true.

"Hey, Annie, wait up!" a familiar voice called. I saw Dawn waving to me from behind a group of laughing kids who were blocking the hall.

"Hi, Dawn. How's it going?" I asked when she finally managed to get over to me. She had her hair up high on her head in a new style. She was wearing a white top tucked into a very short, navy-blue skirt over pale blue tights.

"Listen, the cheerleaders are having a bake sale in the gym," she said breathlessly, staring at the stack of books in my arms. "Ruby and I are meeting down there. Want to join us?"

"I'd really like to," I said, sighing. "But I can't, Dawn. I've really got to get these notes onto my disk. I'm going to be staying late every afternoon."

Dawn made a face.

"No. Really!" I insisted. "I'm so far behind. Especially since my disk was erased."

Dawn waved to someone down the hall. Then she turned back to me. "Why don't you type really fast, then hurry down to the gym?"

"No. No way," I told her.

"Okay. Call you later," she said, giving me a little wave, then turning and hurrying down the hall.

I trudged into the computer lab, lugging my armload of books.

Miss Elwood, the computer instructor, was at her desk in the back of the room, studying a thick software catalogue. She glanced up as I entered, smiled, and returned to her book.

There were a couple of other kids I didn't recognize, typing away at keyboards, their faces illuminated in green from the glow of their monitor screens.

I put down the stack of books beside the computer I always used. It wasn't one of the new Macs. It was an old Apple, but I really liked the keyboard. No one else seemed to like this computer, so it was always free, ready for me to use.

I found my disk in the disk file, carried it over to the old Apple, sat down, and shoved the disk into the drive.

I really enjoyed doing research. I found it strangely satisfying — digging up little bits of information, then putting them in some kind of order. It was sort of like a puzzle. And it was fun to see the pieces come together.

I turned on the power, and the computer hummed to life.

I lowered my fingers to the keys to type in the opening commands to boot the disk.

I felt the first painful jolt as my fingers pressed the keys.

Bright light — like lightning — shot over my hands, with a loud crackle.

I heard a buzz.

Felt another jolt of pain.

Electricity crackled over my hands. Shot through my body.

Gasping, I tried to pull my hands away.

But the crackling blue-white current held me prisoner.

"H-h-h-h — " I tried to call for help. But the current was forcing my entire body to tremble out of control. "H-h-h-h — "

Out of control . . .

The crackling grew louder. The blue-white light snapped around me.

It grew brighter. Brighter.

The pain was so intense!

Then everything went black.

Chapter 17

A thin blue light trailed through the utter blackness.

The light glowed brighter. Brighter.

Cold blue light, ribbon-thin.

It exploded into a wash of bright colors.

I opened my eyes.

Miss Elwood's worried face came into sharp focus.

Everything seemed so bright, so clear. As if all the lights had been turned up. As if the white electricity had given everyone a brighter-than-daylight glow.

"She's opening her eyes," Miss Elwood told someone else in the room.

I slowly realized that I was no longer seated at the computer. Staring up at the ceiling lights above Miss Elwood's frowning face, I saw that I was flat on my back on the floor.

Everything seemed to be vibrating. Pulsing. Buzzing.

"Miss Elwood?"

My voice came out flat, nearly a whisper.

"She's talking," Miss Elwood told someone near the door.

I heard shuffling feet, murmurs, muffled voices.

Miss Elwood peered down at me, her face just a few inches above mine. "Annie, can you hear me?" she asked anxiously.

"Yes." Again, my voice didn't sound like me.

"Can you see me?" Miss Elwood demanded, so close I could smell peppermint on her breath.

"Yes," I told her.

I tried to sit up. But I felt dizzy, so I dropped back down.

Why was everything vibrating like that?

I thought I heard the crackling sound. The crackling of electricity. But it was only in my mind.

I turned my head and saw several other kids and a few teachers huddled against the wall.

"What happened?" I asked.

"You got a bad shock," Miss Elwood said.

"Huh?" I stared up at her. She pulled her head back a little. I felt a little stronger. I sat up.

The lights were dimming to normal. The crackling stopped.

"You got a bad shock. From the computer." She pointed. The old computer had been unplugged, the cord draped over the monitor.

"Those machines aren't supposed to do that," Miss Elwood said.

Right, I thought bitterly. *That's pretty obvious, isn't it!*

"The electricity just shot out from the keyboard," Miss Elwood explained.

I climbed to my feet. I felt strange. Not weak or dizzy.

I felt *crazy*. Really *pumped*.

I felt like running for ten miles. Or putting my fist right through the wall.

It was from all that electricity, I guess.

"Did you touch the plug or something?" Miss Elwood demanded, biting her lower lip.

"Huh-uh," I said. "Only the keyboard."

"I can't understand it," she said, staring at me intently.

I *can*, I thought.

I can understand it.

The anger surged in my chest like a jolt of electricity.

I saw the white light again.

My anger raged through me like a powerful current.

Ruby!

Ruby had tampered with the computer.

I knew it in a burst of angry white light.

That's why Ruby was running down the hall with that wild look on her face.

That's why Ruby ran right past me without seeing me, without stopping.

Ruby had wired the keyboard.

She took that electrical class on Saturdays. That's where she learned how.

And now she had tried to kill me with electricity.

She had tried to kill me to keep me away from Jonathan. To make her threats come true.

She had wired the keyboard. To kill me.

Kill me. Kill me. Kill me.

"Annie — come back!" Miss Elwood shouted.

I didn't even realize that I was running until I reached the hallway.

"Come back!" I could hear her scream.

But I kept running. I couldn't stop myself.

I couldn't stop my rage.

It raced through my body like a powerful jolt of current.

I heard the hideous crackling sound again. I saw the eerie blue light. It filled my eyes, shimmering brighter and brighter as I ran — until it suddenly burst into the brightest, angriest red, so red, so angry, I shut my eyes.

Ruby did it, I told myself.

Her name repeated in my mind until it became an ugly word.

Where was I running?

I'm not sure I knew.

The anger was driving me forward. The red electric anger was moving me blindly through the halls, past rows of lockers, past doorways, all red, all blazing red.

When I burst into the crowded gym, I wasn't sure where I was. Faces came into focus, bright focus. I saw smiling faces. I saw cheerleaders in their uniforms. I saw kids milling about the tables of the bake sale.

I'm here, I told myself. My anger, my *fury*, had brought me here.

To do what?

And then I saw Dawn and Ruby against the tile wall. And standing next to Ruby was Jonathan.

She had one hand on the shoulder of his sweater.

They were laughing.

Their laughter, the hand on his shoulder, her disheveled red hair — it was all too much.

With an angry shriek that I didn't even realize had come from me, I lunged across the gym. Ignoring the startled cries around me, I threw myself on Ruby.

Her eyes bugged out in shock as I wrapped my hands around her throat.

I leapt at her with such force that we both toppled to the floor.

As the red light crackled and buzzed, I wrestled her down.

I heard screams. Loud cries. Alarmed voices.

Red. I saw only red.

Then I felt strong hands on my shoulders, pulling me up, pulling me away.

As the hands held me back, Ruby scrambled to her feet.

She was red-faced, as red as my anger, and her eyes were filled with tears.

I turned to see who had pulled me away. It was Dawn.

"Just chill!" she was shouting in my ear. "Chill, Annie! Just chill!"

Ruby stood hunched over in front of me, her hands pressed against her knees, panting loudly.

The gym buzzed and crackled with excited voices.

With a swift motion, I jerked myself free of Dawn.

Ruby raised herself warily, glaring at me, her chest heaving.

"You tried to kill me!" I screamed at her.

Her face filled with surprise, but she didn't reply.

"But you're not going to scare me away! You're not!" I shrieked.

"Annie, what's your problem?" Ruby snapped, rubbing her throat with one hand. "What is your *problem*?"

"You know what I'm talking about," I said through gritted teeth, lowering my voice as I saw two teachers approaching.

"No, I don't. I *don't*!" Ruby insisted. "You're messed up, Annie. You really are!"

I opened my mouth to say something, but no sound came out. Angrily, helplessly, I turned to Jonathan. He stood staring at me, his hands balled up tensely at his sides.

"Well, say something!" I shouted at him. "Aren't you going to say *anything*?"

His face reddened. All expression seemed to disappear. He stared back at me, a stone face. "Annie, I don't know what's going on," he said.

The teachers were making their way across the gym to see what the fuss was about.

"Jonathan — " I started. But I didn't know what to say, either.

My anger, I realized, had faded. The bright red current that had brought me storming into the gym had vanished, as if someone had pulled the plug.

Now, with everyone staring at me, with everyone talking about me, I felt embarrassed. Humiliated.

"You're messed up, Annie," Ruby repeated. "I mean it. You're really messed up."

With a groan of defeat, I turned and ran.

I pushed my way through a group of gawking kids and kept running.

My chest heaving, my head throbbing, I shoved open the gym doors and raced through them.

I heard Dawn calling me from the gym. But I never looked back.

I ran up the stairs, panting loudly, stumbling, as I climbed. Then I started down the front hall, my sneakers thundering over the hard floor.

I turned into the corridor where my locker was. Some of the lights had been turned out. The hall looked like a dark, empty tunnel.

My loud gasps echoing against the tile walls, I stopped short when a figure stepped out of the darkness.

She moved silently toward me. And when her face came into the light, I uttered a silent gasp of horror.

It was Louisa.

Chapter 18

I stood in the center of the hall and stared at her, my eyes practically popping out of my head, my mouth wide open.

She stopped, too. Her blonde hair caught the light. She was very pale, paler than her photograph.

Pale as a ghost.

She wore a dark green sweater over tan shorts. She had a blue backpack slung over one shoulder.

Louisa, what are you doing here? I thought. *You're dead.*

I suddenly realized I'd forgotten to breathe. I exhaled with a loud whoosh.

"Are you okay?" she asked. Her pale forehead wrinkled in concern.

"I — I don't know," I stammered. I couldn't stop staring at her. I'd never seen a ghost before.

I took a step back, suddenly frightened.

"It's so dark in this hall with most of the lights out," she said. "Don't they usually leave them on?" She had a smooth, soft voice.

I didn't answer her. I just stared in disbelief. The photograph, the sad, sad photograph had come to life.

Louisa had come back.

But how?

"I'm Danielle Powell," she said, shifting the backpack to her other shoulder. "You're new here, right?"

"Huh?"

I was speechless. I couldn't seem to focus on anything. "What did you say your name was?" I managed to ask.

"Danielle," she repeated.

And then she gasped, and all the life seemed to drain from her face. "I'm not Louisa," she said softly, so softly I could barely hear her. She took a few steps toward me, her pale blue eyes suddenly moist. "Is that what you thought? Did you think I was my sister?"

"They never told me she had a sister," I mumbled, still shaken.

"What?" She hadn't heard me. She gazed at me with concern. "Listen, are you feeling okay?"

"I'm sorry, Danielle," I said, shaking my

head as if trying to clear it. "I'm having a really bad day."

"Tell me about it," she replied, rolling her eyes. "I just had to stay late to make up a physics exam."

"I'm Annie Kiernan," I said, starting to recover my wits. "I just moved to Shocklin Falls, and — "

"You're Jonathan's new girlfriend," she said with an odd smile.

"I don't know," I told her. "I haven't really seen him that much. I — "

"You want to get a Coke or something?" she asked, starting toward the door. "Physics exams make me really thirsty. And this dark hall is giving me the creeps. It's like a tomb." She blushed, probably thinking about Louisa.

"Yeah. Great," I said, following after her. "I'll be glad to get out of here, too."

Ruby flashed into my mind. Ruby, glaring angrily at me.

Had I made a fool of myself back in the gym? Or had Ruby really tried to electrocute me?

I tried not to think of it as I followed Danielle out of the building, into the sunlight of a warm spring afternoon. We walked to a small coffee shop a couple of blocks toward town and slid into a red vinyl booth near the back.

"I really want to apologize," I said, after

we'd ordered Cokes and French fries. "I mean, for the way I stared at you. You must've thought I was *nuts!*"

"Yeah, I did," Danielle said, smiling. Her eyes crinkled when she smiled, and a dimple appeared on her right cheek.

I wondered if Louisa had the same dimple.

"I guess I freak a lot of kids out," she said softly, lowering her eyes to the tabletop. "Since I look so much like Louisa. I'm a year and a half older than she was. But people were always mistaking us. I suppose you know what happened to Louisa."

"Yeah. Some of it," I said awkwardly. "I mean Dawn told me the story. I'm so sorry. Really."

"I feel so bad for Jonathan, and Ruby, too," Danielle said. The Cokes arrived, and she took a long sip from the straw.

"Ruby?" I asked, startled.

"Yeah. You know. The three of them went biking that day, the day Louisa . . . died." She took another long sip, nearly emptying the glass.

"I didn't know Ruby went, too," I said, unable to conceal how stunned I was. "Dawn never told me — "

"She was probably protecting Ruby," Danielle said. "You know Dawn and Ruby have been friends since they were tiny tots."

"I'm sorry to be so nosy," I said, spinning my glass between my hands. "You don't have to answer if you don't want to. But" — I took a deep breath — "do you think that Jonathan or Ruby — ?"

I couldn't finish my question.

It was too horrible.

"Do I think they had anything to do with my sister's death?" she finished it for me. She closed her eyes, then shook her head. "No. Maybe. No."

"Danielle, you really don't have to answer," I said, putting my hand on her slender wrist.

"I don't know *what* to think!" she declared emotionally. "I've spent so many nights unable to go to sleep, just thinking and thinking about it."

She slurped up the rest of the Coke. The waitress brought the French fries. Danielle asked for another Coke.

"Jonathan and Louisa were always fighting," she confided to me. "Always. They were always breaking up, then making up. It was a really stormy relationship. But I really don't think Jonathan would *kill* her because of any stupid fight."

"And Ruby?" I asked.

"I think Ruby was jealous of Louisa. I don't

know. I don't know Ruby very well. I think Ruby probably liked Jonathan. A lot. But, come on, Annie. People don't kill people over things like that."

"Someone tried to kill *me*," I blurted out.

"Huh?" She dropped the ketchup bottle. It clattered onto the tabletop, but didn't break.

I told her what had happened to me in the computer lab.

Danielle frowned, wrinkling her pale forehead thoughtfully. "Those old computers," she muttered. "It probably shorted out. You have no proof that someone rigged it up."

I reluctantly agreed. I was instantly sorry that I'd told her about it. I mean, she had enough problems, enough sadness of her own. She didn't need to hear about my problems.

After that, we chatted for a short while, being careful not to talk about anything important. I liked her. She seemed like a really sweet, thoughtful girl. Even though she was so pale and slight, she seemed to have real strength, the strength to deal with all of the sadness she'd experienced.

We lived in different directions, so we said good-bye outside the coffee shop.

The sun was lowering itself in the late afternoon sky, a red ball sinking below the green trees. The air carried the chill of evening.

I gave Danielle a little wave, then stood watching her walk away. She was so light, she seemed to float away, like a pale ghost, disappearing into the cold, blue afternoon.

The ringing phone woke me up late that night.

Still half asleep, I lifted the receiver.

Again, a frightening, raspy voice whispered angrily in my ear:

"Jonathan will kill you, too, if you don't stay away. Jonathan will kill you too."

Whoever it was hung up.

I was wide awake now.

I replaced the receiver.

As soon as I hung it up, the phone rang again.

My hand hovered over the receiver, trembling.

Should I pick it up?

Chapter 19

As my hand hesitated over the phone, something hit me hard in the stomach.

I uttered a silent gasp and leapt to my feet.

To my relief, it was only Goggles. I guess the phone had awakened him.

The phone rang again. Goggles mewed and lowered himself onto my pillow.

I picked up the phone receiver. "Hello?"

"Hi, Annie. It's me."

"Dawn?" I read the time on my clock radio. It was nearly one.

"Did I wake you?"

"It's so late," I said, sitting down on the edge of the bed. I reached out a hand to pet Goggles, but he jumped off the bed.

"I'm sorry," Dawn said, "but I've just been so upset. I've been thinking about you and Ruby all night, Annie. You know. What happened in the gym."

I shivered. The bedroom window was open.

The breeze blowing in was really cold.

"Yeah. What about it?" I muttered, the whole angry scene flashing through my mind.

"Ruby was terribly hurt," Dawn continued. "I've never seen her so hurt. And upset."

"Too bad," I said sarcastically.

"You really should apologize to her," Dawn said.

My mouth dropped open. I was speechless at the suggestion.

"Annie? Are you still there?"

"Apologize to Ruby?" I cried. "Dawn, are you out of your mind? She tried to *kill* me!"

"Annie, listen — "

"She wired the computer keyboard to *electrocute* me!" I screamed, forgetting that I might wake up the rest of the family.

"She couldn't have," Dawn replied softly.

"Huh? What do you mean?"

"Ruby couldn't rig up anything like that."

"What about that electrical class you two are taking?" I demanded.

"We've only had two classes," Dawn told me. "We don't know anything. There's no way Ruby could wire up a computer. She can barely unscrew a lightbulb from a lamp."

"Then *who* did it?" I asked shrilly. I could feel myself going out of control. My throat tightened in anger. And in fear.

"How should I know?" Dawn replied. "It was probably an accident, Annie. But you shouldn't have blamed Ruby. She called me tonight. She couldn't stop crying."

"Boo-hoo," I said nastily. But I was beginning to feel guilty.

This afternoon, I had been so frightened and so angry, I didn't know *what* I was doing. When I ran into the gym, all I could see was bright red. I could've strangled Ruby then. I really wanted to harm her.

But maybe Dawn was telling the truth. Maybe I blamed the wrong person.

"Why are you sticking up for Ruby?" I demanded, pulling the blanket over my bare legs.

"She's my friend," Dawn said. "And she's really not a bad person, Annie. I know you got off to a bad start with her. But Ruby is really okay."

"Well, how come you didn't tell me that Ruby was up at the falls when Louisa died?"

That question caught Dawn offguard.

There was a long silence.

Finally, she answered, speaking slowly, carefully. "It was old news, Annie. I didn't think you needed to know it. I didn't want to turn you against Ruby. I thought all three of us could be good friends."

She sighed. There was another long silence.

"I guess I should tell you the whole story," she said quietly. "Ruby had a thing about Jonathan for a while. I don't think Jonathan was ever seriously interested in her. He just saw her as a friend. But sometimes when he and Louisa were fighting, he'd go out with Ruby. And that's all. After Louisa died, it was all over between them."

"Oh, really?" I said, not intending it to come out so nastily. "Then how come Ruby and Jonathan went out together last weekend?"

"It wasn't a real date," Dawn said. "Really. Ruby told me all about it. At the class on Saturday. It wasn't a date at all."

"Listen, Dawn," I said impatiently, watching the curtains flutter in front of my open window. "Someone is trying really hard to frighten me away from Jonathan. And I think it's Ruby."

"I don't," Dawn replied quickly. "I don't think it's Ruby. No way. For all I know, it could be Jonathan himself."

"Huh?" It was my turn to be caught off-guard.

"What are you *saying*, Dawn?" I demanded, squeezing the phone cord tightly in my free hand. "Jonathan?"

"You don't know him very well," Dawn replied. "Sometimes I think he's really crazy. Maybe even dangerous."

"Jonathan? Dangerous?"

"Maybe."

"Well, I don't know, Dawn. He's real moody, but . . ." I didn't know what to say. "I *will* apologize to Ruby," I told Dawn, changing the subject. "I guess I really owe her an apology. I'll invite her for Saturday night. To my birthday party. It's not really a party. Just sort of an open house. You and Caleb are coming, right?"

"Yeah," she replied. "I mean, I am. I don't know about Caleb. I might break up with him before Saturday. He's just too big a goof." She yawned. "But we've been through that before. I think I have to go to sleep now," she said, yawning again.

I said good-night and we both hung up.

"Goggles? Are you here?" I called softly.

I had an urgent need to hug something.

But the bad cat had run from the room.

Everyone seemed to be having a good time at my birthday open house on Saturday night. Our living room isn't exactly enormous, but no one seemed to mind being jammed in like sardines.

The music was really loud, and the laughter was even louder.

I boiled up a huge pot of spaghetti. And

everyone stood or sat around with their bowls of spaghetti, slurping it up as best they could. It was actually a very funny sight.

Dawn showed up with Caleb. They seemed to be as together as always. I guessed Dawn had changed her mind about breaking up with him during the week.

Ruby showed up, too. She even brought me a present. I could tell when I took it from her that it was a book.

I had called Ruby the morning after my conversation with Dawn and apologized for twenty minutes, begging her forgiveness. I only did it because of Dawn. I was still very suspicious of Ruby, in spite of Dawn saying what a good person she was.

Jonathan seemed very relaxed. I could see he was having a good time, joking with some of his friends, laughing more than I'd ever seen him.

As I passed by him outside the kitchen, he grabbed both my hands and, smiling, started to pull me toward the corner of the living room where some kids were dancing. "Come on," he urged. "I really like this song. Come on. Let's dance."

I started to go with him, but I heard someone knocking on the back door. Jonathan got a pouty look on his face as I pulled away from him and headed through the kitchen to see who was at the back.

"Ryan!" I cried in surprise, pulling open the kitchen door and flicking on the back porchlight.

He looked terribly embarrassed. He fiddled with his glasses, avoiding my eyes. "I — I didn't know you were having a party," he stammered. "I just stopped by to . . . uh . . . say hi. See if you were busy, but . . ."

"Come in," I told him. "It's just an open house. For my birthday. Why don't you stay a while, have some spaghetti?" I pointed to the big, steaming pot on the stove.

I didn't really want Ryan at my party. Actually, he gave me the creeps.

But what could I do? There he was.

He came in, looking very reluctant. I hurried back to Jonathan in the living room.

"The song's over," Jonathan said, still pouting.

"I'll play it again," I said, moving to the CD player.

He grabbed my arm gently. "That's okay. Hey, want to go biking with me tomorrow afternoon? If it's a nice day?"

"Yeah. Sure. I guess," I replied.

Then he surprised me by wrapping his arms

around my waist and lowering his face to mine in a really intense kiss.

I closed my eyes at first and returned the kiss.

When I opened them, I saw Ruby staring at us from across the room, an unhappy frown frozen on her face.

What's her problem? I asked myself silently.

Ignoring her, I kissed Jonathan again.

"What a mess!" my mother cried, her eyes surveying the kitchen.

"It's not as bad as it looks," I said. "It's *worse!*"

Mom and I both laughed.

"Maybe spaghetti wasn't such a great idea," she said, staring at a wide puddle of tomato sauce in the middle of the kitchen linoleum.

"It seemed like a good idea at the time," I sighed.

"I'll change my shoes. Then we'll get to work," Mom said, pushing a strand of blonde hair off her forehead.

"No. Really. You don't have to help," I told her. "You and Dad were so good tonight, hiding up in your room the whole night."

"We *were* good, weren't we?" Mom said, smiling. "But I'll come help you clean up anyway, Annie. Otherwise, you'll be here all night."

She started toward the doorway, then stopped abruptly.

"Hey, you left the spaghetti water on," she said.

"No, I didn't," I insisted. "I turned it off. I remember."

"Well, it's boiling over," Mom said, irritated.

We both made a mad dash to the stove and turned off the burner. The lid was bouncing around on top of the pot, steaming liquid frothing up, running down the sides, onto the stove.

I lifted the lid. "Yuck. What's this white stuff?" I asked.

Bobbing on the top of the boiling water was a large white hunk of cotton.

"How'd this get in here?" I asked, making a face. "What on earth is it?"

I poked it with a long wooden spoon.

As I rolled it over, two blank, blue eyes came into view.

When I finally realized what it was, I started to scream.

It wasn't a hunk of cotton bubbling at the top of the pot.

It was Goggles.

Chapter 20

Jonathan showed up at my house the next afternoon. He came walking into the kitchen, wearing a black-and-yellow sleeveless T-shirt pulled down over black spandex bike shorts.

I looked up from my seat at the kitchen table, surprised to see him. "I told you on the phone I don't feel like riding," I said glumly.

"I know," he replied. "I wasn't going to come. But then I thought it might be good for you to get out of the house. You know. Get some sunshine. Take your mind off . . . what happened."

He put a hand on my shoulder and kept it there. His hand was hot and wet through the sleeve of my top.

When he had called at ten to see what time I wanted to go biking, I'd told him about Goggles. "Who would do that?" I had asked, still too upset to even think about it clearly. "Who would be so cruel?"

"It had to be someone at the party," Jonathan had replied thoughtfully.

Someone at the party.

"I can't go biking today," I'd told him, my voice trembling.

Every time I closed my eyes, I saw Goggles, a bubbling furball, boiled to death in that big pot.

"Okay. I understand," Jonathan replied quietly. "Take it easy, okay?"

But now, three hours later, here he was, standing beside me in the kitchen. I turned and stared up into his startling green eyes. He had a grim, faraway look on his face.

I wondered what he was thinking about.

"It's almost like summer out," he said. "It's really great. Come on out. For a short ride. It'll make you feel better. Really."

I turned my gaze to the golden sunlight pouring in through the kitchen window.

"It'll take your mind off Goggles," Jonathan urged. "Come on. You can't just sit and mope in this kitchen all day. It's too depressing."

"Okay," I reluctantly agreed. I scooted the chair back and stood up. Then I called to my mom to tell her I was going out, and followed Jonathan out the back door.

It was a bright, beautiful day. Everything seemed to shimmer and glow from the bright sunshine. The grass and trees were that amazing fresh green you only see in springtime.

Two robins were fighting over a long earthworm beside the garage. Our neighbors on both sides were noisily mowing their lawns. I held my ears to block out the roar of the power mowers.

We rode side by side along our usual route. When we got past town, we picked up speed. At first, my legs felt as if they weighed a hundred pounds each. But as we continued along the road, I started to gain my usual strength.

It took me a while to realize we were headed for the falls.

We left our bikes on the bike path and walked toward the cliff edge. The water sparkled pure white as it fell. Above us, the sky was solid blue, not a wisp of a cloud in sight.

Jonathan walked right up to the edge and peered down. It always made me so nervous when he did that. I stayed several feet back.

After a few seconds, he turned and came back to me. We both sat down on the ground, the falls roaring beneath us.

I decided to tell Jonathan about how some-

one was trying to scare me away from him. I'd
been thinking about it all night and all morning.

Finally, I'd decided I had to tell him.

He listened to the whole story without moving, a vacant expression on his face. He kept
his eyes toward the cliff edge and didn't react
to a thing I said.

"I think the same person killed Goggles," I
said, finishing the story, my voice breaking.
"But who could it be, Jonathan? Who?"

He didn't reply.

Turning toward me, he locked his eyes on
mine. But he still didn't say anything.

His silence was driving me crazy.

"You *have* to say something!" I demanded.
"You can't just stare at me like that after all
I've told you."

"I don't know what to say," he said finally,
lowering his eyes.

"You know, you can't just be silent all the
time," I continued heatedly, "and never tell
people what's on your mind. I can tell you're
keeping something from me."

He shrugged.

"You've never once mentioned Louisa," I
blurted out.

I think it was the first time I'd mentioned
her name in front of him.

"You've never talked about Louisa once," I continued. "Not once."

He shut his eyes as if trying to shut out my voice.

"I know it's hard for you," I said, softening my tone, seeing the pain on his face. "I know it's hard, but I've got to know, Jonathan. You've got to tell me the truth."

He opened his eyes. "The truth?"

"You've got to tell me what really happened up here that day."

"Now, wait a minute, Annie," he started.

I put a hand on his arm. "No. You have to tell me," I insisted. "You have to tell me the whole story about Louisa. I know you cared about her so much — "

"*Cared* about her?"

His mouth dropped open. He jumped to his feet.

"*Cared* about her?" He stared down at me, his face twisted in excitement. "Are you *crazy*, Annie? *Cared* about her?" Jonathan screamed.

"I *hated* Louisa!" he bellowed. "I hated her so much, *I killed her!*"

Chapter 21

The roar of the falls grew louder, louder — until I felt as if it were roaring inside my head!

And then I suddenly felt as if my head were about to explode.

"I hated her so much, I killed her!"

The words repeated themselves in my mind, over the deafening roar of the sparkling white water beneath us.

Jonathan stared down at me, his expression wild, his features twisted angrily. His hands were balled into tight fists at his sides as he stood over me. Menacingly.

"I hated her so much, I killed her!"

A wave of dread swept over me as I scrambled to my feet.

He had just confessed.

He had just admitted to me that he had killed Louisa.

And now I was here with him. Alone with him.

The only one to share his terrifying secret.

And he was staring at me with that crazed, dangerous look on his face, staring so intensely into my eyes, as if trying to decide what to do next.

As if trying to decide what to do about me.

As if trying to decide whether or not to push me, too.

"I hated her so much, I killed her!"

Why? I wondered.

Why did he do it?

"Jonathan," I said, taking a step back from the cliff edge, away from him. "Jonathan, you . . . pushed Louisa? Over the falls?" My voice sounded tiny and choked.

I wasn't sure he'd heard me over the relentless roar of the rushing water.

But his expression changed. His forehead wrinkled in consternation. His eyes narrowed. "No," he said. "I didn't push her."

I waited for him to offer more, but he lapsed back into silence.

My entire body shivered. I felt ice-cold despite the bright sunshine. I wrapped my arms around me for warmth, for protection.

But I felt totally alone. Totally vulnerable.

"You said you killed her," I repeated.

He shook his head sadly. "Yes. By bringing her up here. If I hadn't brought Louisa here, she wouldn't have died." He let out a groan of pain, of anguish.

"But you didn't push her?" I *had* to know the truth.

He trained his eyes on mine and moved closer to me. "Someone else pushed her," he said. "Someone else."

I stared back at him, searching his eyes, searching his face, trying to tell if what he was telling me was true.

"Someone else," he repeated.

"You mean . . . Ruby?" I asked. "Did Ruby push Louisa?"

Jonathan nodded. "Yes."

Chapter 22

A flock of birds, tiny dark v's high in the sky, flew silently overhead, casting no shadow.

Jonathan took another step toward me.

He was breathing hard. His eyes were narrowed, his jaw clenched tightly.

"Ruby pushed her?" I repeated, not wanting to believe it.

"Yes," he said. "I brought Louisa up here. But Ruby pushed her."

"Liar!"

The voice from the rocks startled us both.

"Liar! You filthy liar!"

We both turned to see Ruby running out from behind the tall pile of granite rocks. She wore a blue midriff top over white tennis shorts. Her red hair flew wildly about her face, which was twisted in a frightening expression of pure rage.

"Ruby, are you still following me?" Jonathan cried angrily. "I told you — "

"Shut up!" she shrieked and shoved him hard in the chest, causing him to stumble back a few steps toward the cliff edge. "Shut up! Shut up! Shut up!"

She tried to push Jonathan again, but he bumped her away with his shoulder.

Glaring at Jonathan, Ruby uttered an angry cry.

"I've been covering up for Ruby all this time," Jonathan said, turning to me.

"Shut up!" Ruby screamed. She turned to me, too. "Don't listen to him. He's a filthy liar!"

"I'm through lying," Jonathan said heatedly. "I'm through covering up for you, Ruby. I can't do it anymore."

"Shut up — I'm warning you!" Ruby threatened.

"In January, I wanted to break up with Louisa," Jonathan explained, eyeing Ruby warily. "Louisa and I never got along. We were always fighting. I brought her up here to tell her. Ruby and I brought her here. We were both going to tell Louisa. Ruby and I had been secretly dating. But, then — "

"Stop it," warned Ruby. "Jonathan, just shut up. Why are you telling her all this?"

"I started to explain to Louisa," Jonathan

continued, ignoring Ruby, staring intently at me, "I started to tell her about Ruby and me. But then Caleb showed up on his bike. I went over there, behind the rocks, to talk to him." He pointed to the rocks.

"And, then," Jonathan's voice broke as he continued. "And then, while I was talking to Caleb, Ruby pushed Louisa and her bike over the falls."

Ruby grabbed my arm and swung me around hard. "Don't listen to him, Annie. It's lies. All lies."

"Ruby — let go of me!" I pleaded, twisting out of her grasp.

"Lies!" Ruby repeated, turning accusingly to Jonathan. "You've been lying since January. Lying to everyone. Even to yourself."

But Jonathan continued to ignore her, talking only to me. "After Ruby killed Louisa, I was sick. I couldn't stand the sight of Ruby. She kept trying to get me to go out with her. But I felt so guilty. So horribly guilty. I didn't want to even *talk* to Ruby again. But she kept following me. She would never leave me alone."

"Liar!"

"Even today!" Jonathan accused. "Even today you're still following me! Leave me alone, Ruby! Leave me alone!"

Ruby uttered another roar of rage. "Liar!"

she cried, giving Jonathan another shove toward the cliff edge. "*You* killed Louisa! *You* pushed Louisa! I didn't! *You* were the one! Admit it!"

Ruby turned to me. "Jonathan, Louisa, and I were up here. We had just started to talk. Then Caleb showed up. Jonathan went back toward the woods to talk to him. Louisa and I were standing by the falls. Then I heard someone calling my name. I thought it was Jonathan. So I left Louisa and hurried to the woods to find him. When I came back, Jonathan was standing on the cliff edge, staring down. And Louisa was gone. Louisa was dead."

"Not true!" Jonathan declared. "I didn't push her—*you* did!"

I cried out as their anger exploded. Jonathan grabbed Ruby furiously around the waist and wrestled her to the ground.

Shrieking at the top of her lungs, she pounded him with her fists, hitting his face, his chest, his shoulders.

"Stop it! Stop it!" I screamed.

But they didn't hear me.

Locked in a bitter struggle, they wrestled, screaming, in the dirt.

"Stop it — *please!*" I cried.

They were rolling in the dirt, rolling toward the cliff edge.

Ruby was pulling Jonathan's hair, pummeling his face, batting his chest with her head.

I ran toward them, screaming, begging them to stop.

They were only a few feet from the cliff edge now.

"Stop it! Stop it, please!" My voice sounded tiny and far away over the roar of the falls.

Ruby scratched her nails down the side of Jonathan's face. The side of his face turned scarlet, and a line of bright red blood appeared.

He cried out in pain.

"Stop it! *Stop* it!" I didn't recognize my shrill, desperate voice.

Jonathan grabbed Ruby's head, twisted it around, and pushed her face into the dirt.

Her hands thrashed the air wildly as she tried to break out of his hold.

They were only inches from the cliff edge now.

"Stop! Please! Look out!"

They couldn't hear me.

They were out of control, I realized. I was watching the explosion of months of guilt, months of suspicion, months of rage.

Jonathan and Ruby hated each other because of the secret they shared.

And their hatred was about to kill them both.

"No!" I cried as Ruby rolled away from Jonathan and, crouched on her knees, pushed him with both hands toward the falls.

I dove toward them, reaching to grab Jonathan's arm and keep him from toppling over the side.

But as I hit the dirt, Jonathan rolled onto his back, reached up, and grabbed Ruby around the knees.

She screamed in protest and broke free.

Then with a breathless snarl of rage, she dove at him.

He rolled underneath her.

And she plunged over the cliff.

Chapter 23

Ruby screamed all the way down.

I didn't hear a splash.

I didn't hear the crack of her body as it slammed onto the jagged black rocks below.

The relentless roar of the falls drowned it out.

The water continued to sparkle and flow. As if it hadn't claimed another victim.

Panting like a wounded animal, Jonathan raised himself to his knees.

Bright red blood rolled down his cheek.

His eyes were wild, confused.

Still on the ground, I stared at the cliff edge in disbelief.

Jonathan was there alone now.

Ruby was gone.

I stared at the spot until my eyes watered over.

I had the urge to run to the edge. To peer

down. To see what had happened to poor Ruby.

But I couldn't move. I couldn't breathe.

I had the sudden, crazy thought that if I just stared at the cliff edge, if I just concentrated hard enough, Ruby would reappear.

I closed my eyes to stop them from watering.

When I opened them, Ruby had not returned.

Only Jonathan remained, gasping, sucking in deep breaths, his chest heaving under his torn, dirt-stained T-shirt.

It took me a long while to realize that the terrified whimpering sounds I heard were coming from me. My entire body shuddered.

Jonathan climbed slowly to his feet, still struggling to catch his breath.

I was on my knees, my arms wrapped around my chest.

The roar of the falls grew louder.

Jonathan stared down at me.

Such an odd expression on his face. Such an odd, hateful expression.

As if he hated me, too.

He took a heavy step toward me, his eyes wild, his jaw clenched tightly.

The blood oozed down the side of his face.

He's a murderer, I realized.

I'm alone now. With a murderer.

He murdered Louisa. He just murdered Ruby.

And now he's coming to murder me.

Get up, Annie, I told myself, feeling cold panic tighten my throat.

Get up! Get up!

Jonathan slowly moved toward me.

But I couldn't stand up.

Chapter 24

"J-Jonathan? What?" I stammered.

My entire body was trembling.

The falls roared angrily in my ears.

He was a murderer.

He wanted to murder me.

I had to get away.

Uttering a terrified cry, I leapt to my feet. I turned and started to run.

I ran right into Dawn.

"Oh!" I cried.

Dawn! She was hurrying toward me, running from the bike path.

"Dawn — thank God you're here!" I cried.

I let out a loud sob of relief and threw my arms around her.

"It's okay now," she said softly. "Really, Annie. It's okay now."

I let her guide me back toward Jonathan, back toward the cliff edge.

"But Ruby — !" I sobbed. "Ruby fell over the side! Did you see?"

"I saw it all," Dawn said softly, soothingly.

Jonathan stood at the cliff edge, hands at his waist. He stared at Dawn suspiciously. "What are *you* doing here?" he asked Dawn nastily.

"I saw it all," Dawn told him. "I was back at the rocks, and I saw everything that happened."

"You mean — " Jonathan started.

"I saw Annie push Ruby over the cliff," Dawn said.

"Huh?" I cried out in confusion. *What* had Dawn just said?

I pulled away from her, but she blocked my path. She took a step forward, her eyes narrowing.

I had no choice. I took a step back, toward the falls.

"I saw Annie push Ruby over the cliff," Dawn told Jonathan.

"No!" I shrieked.

"Then," Dawn continued calmly, ignoring me, speaking only to Jonathan, "Annie tried to push *you* over the side. But Annie slipped, and she accidentally fell herself."

An odd smile formed on Dawn's face. "Isn't that a shame?" she asked Jonathan sarcastically. "Poor Annie."

Chapter 25

Listening to Dawn and her deliberate lies made something inside me snap.

My terror disappeared, replaced by anger.

I felt the red current of anger I had felt that afternoon in the gym.

"Why are you *doing* this?" I demanded of her. "Why are you saying all this? You *know* it isn't true!"

Dawn laughed. "But it *is* true. Isn't it, Jonathan?" She turned back to me, tossing her disheveled black hair behind her shoulder. "At least, that's what Jonathan and I will tell everyone after you're gone, Annie."

Jonathan rubbed his cheek where the blood had turned dark and was starting to cake. "I don't get it, Dawn," he said quietly.

Dawn uttered a moan of frustration. "No, Jonathan. I guess you *don't*!" she exclaimed bitterly. "Well, let me explain it to you. Why do you think I've put up with that idiot Caleb all these months?"

Jonathan didn't answer. He stared back at her, rubbing his wounded face.

"I couldn't stand Caleb," Dawn said angrily, practically spitting the words. "But I stayed with him just to be close to you." She took a deep breath. "After I killed Louisa, I thought that you and I — "

Jonathan and I both let out loud cries of surprise.

"*You* killed Louisa?" Jonathan asked, his face bright red, his eyes revealing deep pain along with his surprise.

Dawn laughed bitterly. "All these months, you and Ruby suspected each other. What a riot. I enjoyed that. I really did."

"But, Dawn — " Jonathan started.

Dawn cut him off. "I thought it would be you and me after that, Jonathan. But you didn't know I was alive. Even after I killed for you. First, Ruby wouldn't let you alone. Then . . ." Dawn raised her eyes to me, her features twisted in hatred.

"Then, Annie came along. With her perfect blonde hair and her perfect little figure. I tried to scare Annie away. I really tried. But . . ."

It had been Dawn all along, I realized. Dawn, who slashed my bike tires, who rigged the computer, who made those threatening calls, who murdered Goggles.

Crazy Dawn.

My friend.

My friend, who was crazy enough about Jonathan to kill for him.

And kill again.

"Enough talk," she said in a low whisper. "Jonathan, say good-bye to Annie."

I stiffened my muscles, readied myself, prepared to duck away from her and run.

But she was faster than I'd imagined.

Before I could react, she lunged forward.

She ran into me, lowering her shoulder like a football lineman, backing me to the edge.

And before I could even cry out in horror, I went sailing over the falls.

Chapter 26

I mean, in that blind second of heart-stopping panic, I *imagined* myself toppling over the falls.

I cried out and sank to my knees on the edge as I realized that Dawn had failed. As I realized that I was safe.

The water rushed loudly below me.

My heart pounded even louder.

I was safe. Safe on the ground. Safe on hard, solid ground.

I raised my eyes to see Jonathan with his arms around Dawn's legs. He had tackled her from behind.

And now he was holding her face down on the ground, pinning her on the ground with both hands as she thrashed and squirmed and tried to free herself.

The sky turned red. Then blue. Then red again.

Was it the red of my anger?

No.

I pulled myself to my feet, blinking against the flashing red light.

The flashing red light of a Shocklin Falls police car.

Two black-uniformed policemen were hurrying toward us across the dirt.

"Throw me over!" Dawn screamed to Jonathan, struggling desperately to get out from under him. "Throw me over, too! I know you want to! I know you hate me enough!"

But Jonathan kept her pinned to the ground until one of the policemen pulled him away and grabbed Dawn's arms.

"How'd you get here?" I stammered to his partner. "I mean, how'd you know we were here?"

"Your friend," he answered flatly, his mustached face completely expressionless.

"Friend?" I stared at him in total bewilderment.

He pointed down, over the falls.

I took a step toward the edge and looked down. An orange-and-white ambulance stood on the near bank of the river.

"She was lucky," the policeman said in the same monotone.

"Ruby?" I cried, staring wide-eyed as two

white-uniformed medics helped someone into the back of the ambulance.

"Yeah. She's got a broken arm. Some broken ribs. But she walked out. She told us you were up here. Good thing, huh?"

I uttered a sigh of relief. Ruby was going to be okay.

When I turned back, both policemen were leading Dawn to their car. She was still struggling. Still screaming hysterically, "Throw me over! Throw me over, too!"

Jonathan made his way to me and put his arm around my shoulder.

"You two need a ride home?" one of the policemen called, holding the driver's door open.

"No. We can ride our bikes," Jonathan answered.

"Get cleaned up. Then come to the station. We'll need statements from you both," the policeman instructed. He slid behind the wheel and slammed the door hard.

His partner was in the back seat with Dawn, who was still screaming and crying.

A few seconds later, the police car squealed away.

His arm around my shoulder, Jonathan led me back to our bikes. He sighed wearily. "Who says nothing ever happens in small towns?"

I shook my head. "I think it's going to get a

lot more boring from now on," I replied.

"Hope so," he said quietly.

Then he let his bike fall to the ground as he put his arms around me, pulled me close, and kissed me.

He was sweaty and smelly. He was covered in dirt, and his face was caked with dried blood.

I kissed him back.

I hardly even noticed.

About the Author

R.L. STINE is the author of more than three dozen mysteries for young people, all of which have been best-sellers. Recent Scholastic horror titles include *The Baby-sitter III* and *The Hitchhiker*.

In addition, he is the author of two popular monthly series: *Goosebumps* and *Fear Street*.

R.L. lives in New York City with his wife, Jane, and thirteen-year-old son, Matt.

THRILLERS

Nobody Scares 'Em Like R.L. Stine

THRILLERS

R.L. Stine

- ☐ MC44236-8 The Baby-sitter $3.50
- ☐ MC44332-1 The Baby-sitter II $3.50
- ☐ MC46099-4 The Baby-sitter III $3.50
- ☐ MC45386-6 Beach House $3.25
- ☐ MC43278-8 Beach Party $3.50
- ☐ MC43125-0 Blind Date $3.50
- ☐ MC43279-6 The Boyfriend $3.50
- ☐ MC44333-X The Girlfriend $3.50
- ☐ MC45385-8 Hit and Run $3.25
- ☐ MC46100-1 The Hitchhiker $3.50
- ☐ MC43280-X The Snowman $3.50
- ☐ MC43139-0 Twisted $3.50

Caroline B. Cooney

- ☐ MC44316-X The Cheerleader $3.25
- ☐ MC41641-3 The Fire $3.25
- ☐ MC43806-9 The Fog $3.25
- ☐ MC45681-4 Freeze Tag $3.25
- ☐ MC45402-1 The Perfume $3.25
- ☐ MC44884-6 The Return of the
                Vampire $2.95
- ☐ MC41640-5 The Snow $3.25
- ☐ MC45682-2 The Vampire's
                Promise $3.50

Diane Hoh

- ☐ MC44330-5 The Accident $3.25
- ☐ MC45401-3 The Fever $3.25
- ☐ MC43050-5 Funhouse $3.25
- ☐ MC44904-4 The Invitation $3.50
- ☐ MC45640-7 The Train $3.25

Sinclair Smith

- ☐ MC45063-8 The Waitress $2.95

Christopher Pike

- ☐ MC43014-9 Slumber Party $3.50
- ☐ MC44256-2 Weekend $3.50

A. Bates

- ☐ MC45829-9 The Dead
                Game $3.25
- ☐ MC43291-5 Final Exam $3.25
- ☐ MC44582-0 Mother's Helper $3.50
- ☐ MC44238-4 Party Line $3.25

D.E. Athkins

- ☐ MC45246-0 Mirror, Mirror $3.25
- ☐ MC45349-1 The Ripper $3.25
- ☐ MC44941-9 Sister Dearest $2.95

Carol Ellis

- ☐ MC46411-6 Camp Fear $3.25
- ☐ MC44768-8 My Secret
                Admirer $3.25
- ☐ MC46044-7 The Stepdaughter $3.25
- ☐ MC44916-8 The Window $2.95

Richie Tankersley Cusick

- ☐ MC43115-3 April Fools $3.25
- ☐ MC43203-6 The Lifeguard $3.25
- ☐ MC43114-5 Teacher's Pet $3.25
- ☐ MC44235-X Trick or Treat $3.25

Lael Littke

- ☐ MC44237-6 Prom Dress $3.25

Edited by T. Pines

- ☐ MC45256-8 Thirteen $3.50

Available wherever you buy books, or use this order form.

Scholastic Inc., P.O. Box 7502, 2931 East McCarty Street, Jefferson City, MO 65102

Please send me the books I have checked above. I am enclosing $_____ (please add
$2.00 to cover shipping and handling). Send check or money order — no cash or C.O.D.s please.

Name _____ Birthdate _____

Address_____

City _____ State/Zip_____
Please allow four to six weeks for delivery. Offer good in the U.S. only. Sorry, mail orders are not
available to residents of Canada. Prices subject to change.   T193